SKETCHY BEHAVIOR

SKETCHY BEHAVIOR

Erynn Mangum

ZONDERVAN®

ZONDERVAN.com/
AUTHORTRACKER
follow your favorite authors

We want to hear from you. Please send your comments about this book to us in care of zreview@zondervan.com. Thank you.

ZONDERVAN

Sketchy Behavior
Copyright © 2011 by Erynn Mangum O'Brien

This title is also available as a Zondervan ebook.
Visit www.zondervan.com/ebooks.

Requests for information should be addressed to:
Zondervan, *Grand Rapids, Michigan* 49530

Library of Congress Cataloging-in-Publication Data

Mangum, Erynn, 1985–
    Sketchy behavior / Erynn Mangum.
        p. cm.
        Summary: As part of an art class assignment, high school junior Kate unwittingly
    sketches a wanted murderer, propelling her into instant celebrity and extreme
    danger while her parents fret and police provide constant protection.
        ISBN 978-0-310-72144-4 (softcover)
        1. Murder—Fiction. 2. Artists—Fiction. 3. Police—Fiction. 4. Celebrities—
    Fiction. 5. High schools—Fiction. 6. Schools—Fiction. 7. Family life—Missouri—
    Fiction. 8. Missouri—Fiction. I. Title.
    PZ7.M31266532Ske 2011
    [Fic]—dc23

                                                                        2011013223

Cover still-life illustration: Connie Gabbert
Additional cover images: iStockphoto.com and Shutterstock.com
Interior design and composition: Greg Johnson/Textbook Perfect

Printed in the United States of America

11 12 13 14 15 16 /DCI/ 22 21 20 19 18 17 16 15 14 13 12 11 10 9 8 7 6 5 4 3 2 1

For my sweet little family—my husband, Jon, and my son, Nathan. I love you both more than I can put into words.

Chapter One

I GUESS IT WOULD MAKE SENSE THAT SOMEONE LOOKING death in the face would be shaking violently. I just always figured suicides were a little bit calmer.

My friend Madison Hanson was perched precariously on the edge of the one and only bridge in South Woodhaven Falls. And while the name sounds impressive, the Falls, I think, refer more to the direction gravity flows than any large quantity of water. A river about five feet in depth and about thirty feet across was directly below us.

Enough to get her wet. Not enough to kill her. Which was why I was more concerned about Madison's essay — which counted toward a fourth of her final grade in English and was most likely in the backpack strapped onto her — getting washed away in the muddy water than I was about her imminent end.

"Maddy, what are you doing?" I asked as casually as I could. I kept walking at a nonthreatening pace toward the railing. She was on the other side, hands behind her holding on to the rail.

"It's over, Kate." She sniffed and I saw tears coursing down her freckled cheeks. Madison, in any other circumstance, was really cute. Coppery-red hair, almost-violet blue eyes, on the tall-ish side.

"What's over?"

"Me and Tyler." Her voice was trembling almost as much as she was.

Figures.

I have this theory about guys and it goes like this: Until they reach the age of about thirty-two, they're not even worth associating with, much less dating. All you get is a bunch of tear-soaked Kleenex, awkwardness for everyone around you when you pass in the hallway after your inevitable breakup, and apparently, suicidal tendencies.

This was where I would like to have started the "I told you so" monologue, because I did tell her so, but I didn't have time for that.

Madison was still on the wrong side of the railing, after all.

"Maddy, Tyler's a jerk."

She sniffed. I got a little closer.

"But even if he wasn't a jerk, no one is worth you jumping into the Falls." *And ruining your A+ in English.*

Blinking like crazy, Maddy croaked out, "I know."

"So why are you about to jump?"

She shook her head. "I didn't know what else to do, Kate. I hate feeling like this."

My dad is an engineer. And as such, he has very few spontaneous emotions left inside him, because they try to breed those out of potential engineers freshman year. Deep down, I thought this was why nerds are so often picked on — God knows that someday one of them will have to make a life-or-death decision about leaving a man on the moon, or how to dig out a town covered by an avalanche, or whether or not to nuke a communist country, and they'll have to do it all with zero emotions and a hundred and thirteen percent logic.

All that to say, Dad has a little saying that he told me from the time I was six years old: "Basing a decision on a feeling is like trying to balance an egg on your head while you're on a pogo stick. It doesn't turn out well for you or the egg."

Which was when my mom, who has a psych degree and bases everything on feelings, would say, "No, if you base a decision off of a feeling, it's like holding the egg steady in your hand while on the

pogo stick. All you're left with is the feeling of accomplishment."
And then my parents would argue for the next ten minutes.

My childhood was interesting.

I wasn't sure if Madison would benefit from either of my parental unit's sayings, so I came up with my own.

"Maddy, life is like an egg."

She frowned and looked at me for the first time. "What?"

"When life feels broken and the heat gets turned up, just
remember: You're being made whole again."

"What are you talking about?"

Okay, so it was a bad saying. I'd have to work on that.

"Could you just come back to this side of the railing?" I asked
her. "It's cold, school starts in twelve minutes, and you need a
Kleenex."

She rubbed at her nose with the back of her hand, which was
quite disgusting. "If I go to school, I'll have to look at him all day."

"No, you won't. You don't even have a class with Tyler."

She sighed. "But he comes by my locker every break."

"That's because you were dating, not because he had classes
down that hall."

Her shoulders fell and the tears started again. "But we're
not anymore, are we?" Her voice reached an impossible decibel
level at the end of that sentence. A beagle started wailing in the
distance.

"Please just come with me? I'll guard you the whole time. You
won't even know he existed. Besides, you need to make Tyler think
that you're even better off without him than you were with him."

She looked at me again. "Better off?"

"Vindication, Madison Hanson. Let Tyler know that he can be
the big mean football player all he wants. You are better than him."

Slowly, she climbed back over the railing. "Better off," she
mumbled again.

"Much better off." I wrapped an arm around her shoulders and
tried to push our speed a notch faster. I hadn't been late to class in

exactly six days. Considering that the principal, Mr. Murray, has had it out for me for the entirety of my two and a half years at SWF High, it would be in my best interest to be on time.

We made it by thirty-four seconds. The bell rang just as I gave Maddy one last hug. "You're better without him."

"Right." The red splotches on her face were still tattling her breakdown this morning, but her eyes looked clearer. As clear as bloodshot blue eyes could look.

I turned to run to my locker down the hall.

This year being my junior year, I got to pick from a better-rounded list of electives. Which is why I dumped my backpack in my locker, grabbed my sketchpad and pencils, and hightailed it to art, my preferred elective. I'd always been good at drawing and SWF High's art teacher, Miss Yeager, was probably one of the best teachers at the school. She was twenty-six, extraordinarily attractive, and liked to push us to be more detailed.

I plopped into my seat right as the second bell rang. There were fifteen of us in art class, all gathered around four tables that faced the front of the room.

"Good morning, guys." Miss Yeager had a balding, middle-aged man with a paunch seated in front of us. His only redeeming physical quality was his emerald-like green eyes.

"This is your test subject," Miss Yeager said. "I want you to draw him how *you* see him. You'll have the entire class period for this. Work quickly. Begin now."

I set my sketchpad in front of me and pulled out a soft-leaded pencil. To my right, Allison Northing was scraping big, dramatic strokes on the page. She drew the way she talked. On my left was Justin Walters, who has never spoken to me once in all of my life, but whom I'd been sitting next to in class for the last two months at SWF High. He was lightly running the pencil over the page in wispy little lines.

I stared at the man. Late forties. Wrinkles crisscrossed his forehead. His hair was cut short, embracing the thinning instead of hiding from it. I decided I liked that quality. His lips were thin, his nose slightly crooked like he broke it when he was younger, and like I said earlier, his eyes were stunning.

Smaller shoulders, the paunch, the legs that barely filled out his gray dress slacks ... I got the feeling he was a go-to guy the higher-ups turned to, either at a mathematical company or government-run organization.

"Kate." Miss Yeager was suddenly beside me. "You haven't drawn anything."

"I'm still looking," I told her. "What does he do for a living?"

"What do you think he does?"

"I think he works for the government in environmental law."

Miss Yeager just looked at me. "Catch me afterward, okay, Kate?"

I nodded, biting my lip as she left. Probably another slap on the wrist for buying into stereotypes. Could I help it that the man looks like he does?

Silent Justin looked over at me as Miss Yeager left and then back at his sketchpad. A faint head was appearing on his paper.

I picked up my pencil.

It wasn't enough to merely draw the man — anyone could do that. You had to draw what was *behind* the man, and I didn't mean the chalkboard. What drove him? What captivated him? What made him get up every day?

These are what led to the wrinkles, the balding, the bad sense of fashion.

By the end of the hour, I had a decent sketch of the man's head and shoulders. The bell rang, and Miss Yeager had us applaud our subject and let him exit first. Then she dismissed us.

I waited until everyone left before I walked over to where she was pushing the man's chair back against the wall.

"You wanted to see me?"

She sat on her desk and folded her hands together. "Carl Thompson is a lawyer specializing in defending the aquatic and biological programs implemented by the government."

"I was right?" Now I was surprised.

"How did you know that?"

"You could tell he worried a lot, he had calluses only on his right hand, which meant he wrote a lot but he didn't work outside, he looked tired ..." I shrugged. "I don't know."

Miss Yeager smiled at me. "I'm excited to see where you take this, Kate. Better run if you're going to make the next class."

I nodded and left. The rest of the day passed in a blur. I checked on Madison about forty-three times and each time she seemed sadder and sadder.

Poor Maddy.

I got home and Mom was already there, pulling out a package of chuck steak. "Hi, Kate," she said, laying it on the counter. "How was school?"

"Fine." The perfunctory answer. "How was work?"

Mom sighed, cutting open the package with a knife. "I swear, Kate, ninety percent of the people I see have absolutely nothing wrong with them." She paused and then waved the knife at me. "But you breathe a word of that to your dad, it's your head."

I held my hands up. "Yes, ma'am."

"Good. Go feed Lolly."

I dropped my backpack on the floor and started yelling. "Lolly! Lolly!"

Our big, black Labrador came running, looking all sleepy eyed. "Was someone napping?" I cooed at her.

She was named Lolly because when we got her as a puppy, she

had this big pink tongue that just lolled all over the place. She still did.

It was gross, but we all still loved her anyway.

"And Kate?" Mom called, as I dumped a big cup of food in Lolly's bowl.

"Yeah?"

She came around the corner and looked at me. "I want you to keep the doors locked whenever you are at home by yourself. Apparently, there's some guy they're calling John X who has committed three murders. One in Warren County, one in St. Charles County, and one in Franklin County."

All surrounding counties to St. Louis County, where we lived.

"Statistically, the odds are outrageously low that he would pick our house for his next target," I told Mom.

"Statistics or not, keep the doors locked."

"Yes, ma'am."

My family had dinner at 5:32 every single night.

My dad liked it because three and two make five, so he found it funny in his weird engineer sense of humor. My mom tried for 5:30 every night but always ran two minutes late.

We sat at the table, and it was just the three of us. We still left a chair there for my older brother, Mike, but ever since he moved to California for school he'd been home twice.

But his chair was still there. "Just in case," Mom always said.

"In case what? He flies home in the middle of a semester?" I asked. Mike was following in our dad's footsteps and becoming an engineer. He was not going to leave in the middle of classes that intense.

"Just in case."

And so we left the chair.

As was the custom she borrowed from my grandmother, my mom held both hands out for the prayer. Dad grudgingly put his fork down. "God, bless the food. Amen," he mumbled. "Kate, what did you do in school today?" he asked immediately after.

Mom sighed.

"Well, we drew a guy."

"I meant math. What did you do in math today?"

"Algebra. Same as yesterday."

"Are you understanding it?"

"Yes."

He nodded. "Good girl. See, Claire? Both kids are well on their way to becoming engineers. Keep the Carter name going."

"I thought reproducing kept a name going, not becoming an engineer," I said. "Some people might consider those mutually exclusive, actually."

Dad rolled his eyes. Mom laughed.

"However, this one is sarcastic," he said, pointing to me.

I hated it when Dad talked like I wasn't there.

Dad had this grand illusion that I wanted to be an electrical engineer. When, in all reality, I wanted to be an artist. But *artist* is on the same playing field as a car wash worker or a gift wrapper in the mall as far as my dad is concerned.

We finished dinner, and I started my three hours of homework. I closed my last book just in time to change into my pajamas.

I snuggled under the covers, turned out the light, and sighed. Same as always, always the same.

If I'd known then that my life would never be the same again, maybe I wouldn't have been so depressed by that thought. I drifted to sleep slowly.

Chapter Two

CRISPIX HAS TO BE THE BEST CEREAL EVER. IT IS LIKE A race to see who wins breakfast — will you get them all eaten before they get soggy? Or will they win out when your dumb dog puts her giant head on your lap and slobbered all over your brand-new skirt?

"Lolly!" I shouted, mashing at her head until she finally moved her big drooly face. "No!" I looked down and there was a big huge patch of slime oozing on my skirt.

Fabulous.

"What's wrong, Kate?" Mom asked, running into the kitchen. It was nearly eight and Mom was trying to put in her earrings while simultaneously pouring her coffee into a travel mug.

It didn't work out too well.

"Crumb!" Mom said, which is her version of swearing. She swiped at the coffee blob on the counter before looking at me. "Sorry, Katie-Kin, I have an appointment at eight fifteen."

She kissed me on the forehead and left, yelling, "Lock the doors!" behind her.

The house was completely silent. And there was still a big slimy splotch on my skirt.

When I was a kid, I once read a story about this little girl who was an only child. Her parents worked and she had to walk four miles home from school every day by herself, and she made up all these adventures.

Mom said that the little girl must have had some version of schizophrenia brought on by the stress of being six and having to stay alone all the time. Dad said that instead of having "adventures," she could have been doing her homework so she could have skipped a few grades and left her loser parents behind while she went to college sooner.

I said, "Hey, Dad, I'm home a lot by myself."

And Dad said, "I think I still have some of my old calculus textbooks in the garage."

I never said another word about being home alone after that. Dad has been known to bring flash cards to the table.

So I cleaned up my bowl of soggy Crispix and decided to go hungry rather than pour another bowl. And I exchanged the slobbery skirt for jeans.

This was why I never looked cute at school.

Not like it really mattered whether I looked cute or not. We had to run three miles every day in gym. Our crazy gym teacher, Mr. Hannigan, told us that the most responsible thing we can do for our human bodies is run. And when he said run, he meant run until your feet were bleeding and you were coughing for mercy.

But when we pleaded and cried for mercy, he just told us this story about a woman who was saved from some horrible avalanche or mudslide or whatever because she was like this long-distance running champion. And then Mr. Hannigan told us we would all die in the mudslide.

I might die in the mudslide, but when they uncovered my preserved body thousands of years later, they wouldn't find calluses so deep on my feet that they hadn't even started decomposing.

I got to school with a few minutes to spare, so I headed on into art. It was so early that Miss Yeager wasn't even in the room yet.

How come our principal, Mr. Murray, couldn't see me now?

I sighed and plopped into my seat.

Silent Justin was already there. He was sitting there with his sketchpad and pencils all laid out on the table and two erasers on each side of the pad.

"Good morning, Justin," I said.

I thought he grunted, but I guess I'd never know.

Supposedly, Justin didn't always used to be silent. I've heard that all freshman and sophomore years, he was like the school chatterbox. But then this year he walked through the doors to SWF High's first day of school without saying a thing, and nobody had heard a word from him since.

Maddy said that she thinks Justin joined some cult during the summer that made him take a vow of silence.

And then my friend Aubrey said she heard that Justin went to Bosnia or somewhere all weird like that and he ate the food and his tongue got all infected and they had to amputate it.

I'd seen him lick his lips in art class, so I was pretty sure he still had a tongue.

I looked over at him and watched him stare at his sketchpad, at the chalkboard, at the lights, and back at his sketchpad.

"So did you hear about this John X guy?" I asked.

Allison Northing slid into her seat just then. "Hi, guys. Oh my gosh, I heard that the school board decided to repaint all the lockers a horrible green color next year, can you believe that? I mean, green. Green? Our school colors are black and red! It totally doesn't fit."

She pulled her sketchpad and pencils out while she talked. Allison has always been slightly fascinated with the lockers. Every time we had to draw something freestyle, she drew a row of lockers.

Everyone went through an "Awed with the Lockers" phase when we first got to SWF High, because our one and only junior high did not have lockers, but still. It had been three years — maybe she could start finding other stuff more interesting.

Justin just looked at her. I opened my mouth to be polite and respond, but Miss Yeager walked in right then.

"Okay, class, get settled." She had this super-excited look on her face and her cheeks were all flushed like she just made a homemade organic face mask with strawberries. My mother said that the antioxidants in strawberries could do wonders for your skin.

Miss Yeager said, "I have a very important visitor here today. We're going to be discussing how art can be used in the real world and so I asked Detective Masterson to share a little bit about the field of criminal sketches."

She turned and nodded to the doorway, where a tall guy who looked vaguely like a tougher and less-girly-looking Orlando Bloom stood.

That explained the strawberry face mask.

"Uh, hello," Detective Masterson said. He stepped all the way inside the classroom and took the seat of horror in front of the class. Pete Faraelli picked up his pencil to start sketching him and Miss Yeager told him not to.

"We're not sketching Detective Masterson, Peter. You can put the pencil down."

"Right, right, right," Detective Masterson said. "Don't draw me." Only he said it like *don't drawl me*, because Detective Masterson was apparently not from around here.

Missourians had their own weird way of saying things, but we didn't stretch words out that weren't meant to be stretched.

"So I'm supposed to, uh, talk about criminal sketches. I'm a detective with the SWF police, but I actually spent my first five years with the force doing criminal sketches. Kelly ... uh, I mean, Miss Yeager, asked me to come down here and give a little example of what a criminal sketch artist would do."

He looked nervously at Miss Yeager, and she smiled too brightly. Miss Yeager was very passionate and excited about art, but she was not usually overdramatic about it.

"Yes," she said. "And today we have a special exercise, so everyone get your pencils ready." She looked expectantly at Detective

Masterson. "Would you like to explain a little bit of the nuts and bolts of this procedure?"

"Yeah," Detective Masterson said. "Forensic sketch artists, or criminal sketch artists, are usually part of the interview team when we are talking to witnesses. Uh, you need to know how to ask good questions, because usually the witnesses are so emotionally battered they can't really think straight."

"Wow," Miss Yeager said.

Allison raised her hand. "You mean questions about the bad guy?"

Detective Masterson almost flinched at the words *bad guy*. "Yeah. Uh, so, I'm going to show you a quick demonstration, and then Miss Yeager is going to have you guys do an exercise, I think."

Miss Yeager nodded. "Yes, that's right."

Detective Masterson picked up a Sharpie and walked over to the huge sketchpad that covered almost one side of the classroom. "Typically, you want to start with the gender and an approximate age. Next, work your way down from the forehead to the chin, ending with the details."

He wrote each point out on the paper. "If you're observant and you're skilled at drawing, this can be a great job. Uh, I had a lot of fun with this back when I was forensic sketch artist. You feel like you're really contributing to the case, you know? I once helped slam a guy who used to be a pharmacist and then sold drugs on the black market."

I raised my hand. "Better money?"

Detective Masterson nodded. "Fewer hours too."

"More nights and weekends, though," I said.

"True." He gave me kind of a half-grin. "So, I think you guys are going to do some kind of a practice of this."

"Yes, you are going to have a chance to practice this." Miss Yeager picked up a folder from her desk. "I want you all to pay attention and do your best. This is a very valid field for those of you who are talented at art."

"Definitely valid field," Detective Masterson hummed.

Miss Yeager started reading. "Male. Around thirty-five."

Allison immediately started drawing.

I kept listening.

"Short dark hair, widow's peak. Wide forehead. Wide eyebrows. Brown eyes. Five o'clock shadow and a square chin. High cheekbones."

Silent Justin began sketching.

"Nose is long, but not skinny. Lips are thin, but not too thin." Miss Yeager looked at me now. I glanced back, but mostly I just kept staring at the floor in front of Detective Masterson's shoes, listening.

Miss Yeager continued. "Eyes are small in comparison to the rest of his face. Wears wire-framed glasses."

Allison began erasing.

Miss Yeager looked around the room and everyone was already sketching. Except for me.

"Do you need to know anything else, Kate?" she asked.

"Teeth. Are they straight?"

Detective Masterson looked at the paper Miss Yeager was holding. "Doesn't say." He looked back at me. "But they didn't mention the teeth either when it came to the pharmacy school guy."

I nodded. "Pharmacy school is expensive."

"Nothing compared to braces." He shrugged. "So I imagined straight teeth. Think about the guy's face and then see what comes to your mind."

I closed my eyes.

Pharmacy school was stuck in my head. Mike had a friend who wanted to go to pharmacy school. He was a little straggly guy who looked for all the world like he would blow away with the next windstorm. He always had his hands in his pockets and he talked with a permanent *um* sound. "Um-hi, um-Mrs. um-Carter, um-Mike um-invited um-me um-for um-dinner."

It got annoying.

Dad told Mike that if he ever brought "Um-Chris" back to dinner, we would need a full day's warning.

I started sketching.

I decided to start with his chin. Square chin. Not too many guys have square chins anymore. I like square chins.

I snuck a quick peek and, yup, Silent Justin had a square chin.

For a person to have a square chin and high cheekbones, they would need a seriously dramatic jawline. So I gave the sketch a dramatic jawline. And sprinkled it with some of the five o'clock shadow Miss Yeager mentioned. Sort of à la Matt Damon.

The bell was ringing way too soon.

"Okay, class, please turn in your drawings before you go," Miss Yeager said. She and Detective Masterson spent the whole class quietly whispering.

She still looked like she had on the strawberry face mask.

"So cute," Allison hissed, nodding toward Miss Yeager before she left to go turn in her paper.

I packed up my pencils.

It wasn't that I *didn't* think it was cute. It's just I thought it was overrated. Look at what happened with Maddy and Tyler. Detective Masterson could have been over the age of thirty-two and therefore dateable for Miss Yeager, but still. Was it really worth it?

I had no good luck with guys. My one dating experience was labeled "Do Not Speak of Ever Ever Ever."

So. I didn't speak of it. Ever.

I handed my paper to Miss Yeager.

She smiled at me. "Thanks, Kate."

"You're welcome, Miss Yeager. You are the best teacher at this school. I appreciate your honest desire to teach us the proper techniques for art."

Miss Yeager narrowed her eyes at me, but flushed more. "Compliments don't buy A's."

"But they might buy lunch," I said, nodding to Detective Masterson.

She blushed even more, and this time the detective joined her.

"Kate!" Miss Yeager gasped as I left.

The hallway between classes is always packed. South Woodhaven Falls was quickly becoming one of the best, albeit smallest, suburbs of St. Louis.

I pushed slowly through the throng and finally ended up at my locker. All around me people were talking on cell phones or laughing with their friends.

I grabbed my algebra book.

My mother was always concerned that at school I was a loner. I told her that there were not very many logical people left in my school to talk to, which was when Dad busted into the hallelujah chorus. When I was a freshman, I hung out with all of the juniors and seniors.

Now I was a junior, and all the seniors were so wrapped up in what the theme of prom was going to be, we had nothing in common.

I told Mom that I knew Maddy.

Which was why Mom sent me to that church camp last summer. She said I needed to "make more friends" and "spend a week in a wholesome environment." Really, I thought Mom and Dad just wanted the house to themselves for a few days and the only other camps I could have gone to were for kids with eating disorders or disabilities. Both fine and good purposes, but I didn't fit into either one of those categories.

The Christian camp wasn't bad. I didn't make a ton of new friends. The guy who led it kept harping on all of us to read our Bible more and stuff like that. I read my Bible the camp handed to us every day for a week after I got home.

It didn't make very much sense. I didn't really know where to start, so I started in Leviticus, because I thought that was a weird-sounding word.

I was hoping it was just a poor choice on my part, because if the whole Bible was written like that, I didn't understand why there were so many churches around.

Mom and Dad weren't really religious, per se. It wasn't that I didn't believe in God. I just didn't know what to believe. Some people claimed "God is love" and all that jazz so He sounded like a heavenly Santa Claus, but then others talked about "God is just" and "God is everywhere" and "We are all gods."

It got confusing. And to be honest, I didn't spend that much time thinking about it.

Kyle Barlett bumped into me right as I was walking through the door to algebra.

"Oh," he said, like he just hit a brick wall. He started rubbing his arm like he was going to get a bruise or something now. I was not that solid — I thought he was being a little dramatic. But I kept my mouth shut.

"Sorry, Kate. Didn't see you there."

Then he looked at me real quick in the eyes and darted out the door.

Kyle Bartlett was in that category of "Do Not Speak of Ever."

Actually, he was a major player in that category.

But, like the category title said, I didn't speak of it. Ever.

Chapter Three

MADDY CAUGHT ME AS I WAS DIGGING IN MY BACKPACK for my car keys. When I turned sixteen, Mom and Dad bought themselves a car and they let me borrow it. It was a 1962 Volvo and was a puke greenish-yellow color.

Dad said it was so boys would like me for who I was rather than what I drove. Mom said she didn't know Dad was buying that car, and she thought it would be a horrendous blow to my self-esteem.

I didn't really mind the car as long as it started. So most of the time, I didn't mind it. But I'd had to catch a ride home with Maddy four times in the past two months.

"So, Kate, I told Tyler that, like, if he wanted to break up with me then whatever, because there was totally someone better out there for me," she said. She flipped her copper hair over her shoulder.

Maddy was one of those friends who sometimes intimidated you as far as looks went. She was tall, had the gorgeous hair, the perfect complexion.

Me? I broke out at least once a month, my hair was supposed to look like Reese Witherspoon's hair in *Sweet Home Alabama*, but it flipped out all weird, unlike hers. And I was five foot one. And my hair was probably the most boring shade of brown there is.

She liked to tell me how lucky I was to be shorter than all the guys at school and how I never had to worry about running into things with my head.

Ever noticed how people who give advice about being short are never short? Sorry, but if you've never had to call the dorky bagging boy at Tim's Grocery to help you with the Fritos on the top shelf, you should keep the advice to yourself.

I found my keys and looked up at Maddy. "Well, that's good."

"Yeah."

I tossed my backpack over to the passenger seat.

"So, can I come study with you this afternoon?" Maddy asked.

I looked up at her again as I started to climb into my car. This would be the third time this week.

And it was only Wednesday.

Maddy was one of those students who didn't even need to study and could still pull straight A's. Evidenced by her lack of studying capabilities. When she came over to study, she would spend the whole time talking, watching E!, and filing her nails.

But the house did get quiet with just me and Lolly before Mom and Dad got home, so I always said okay. "Okay," I said. I slid into the Volvo. "See you at the house."

"Great! Thanks, Kate!" She ran to her brand-new, jet-black Tahoe.

The differences between us just kept getting more and more glaring.

It took three tries, but the Volvo started and I drove the few minutes back to my house. Lolly was barking and turning in circles when Maddy and I walked in.

"You really need to see more human contact," I told Lolly.

We settled on the couch. Maddy grabbed the remote and turned on the TV to E! like I knew she would.

I dumped my books and notebooks onto the coffee table.

"Want anything to drink?" I asked her.

"Is your mom still on the health kick?"

Unfortunately, yes. I nodded.

"I'll have water then. No offense to your mom, but that green tea lemonade or whatever it was, was pretty nasty."

I didn't disagree with Maddy. The green tea lemonade tasted like leaves. When you swallowed, there was still this powder-coating stuff all over your tongue. Mom said it was all the vitamins from the green tea. I said it felt like my tongue had a shower cap on it.

I got us two waters and sat down on the floor, pulling my algebra book over.

"Here," Maddy said. "I brought contraband." It was a package of Nutter Butters and I grinned.

"Thanks!"

We sat there crunching. I was focused on reading the homework assignment. Maddy was focused on Ryan Seacrest, who was rattling off the day's "news."

"Michelle Moriega celebrated her birthday last night with two hundred of her best pals at one of the swankiest nightclubs in New York City ..."

I tuned him out after that. I was concentrating on finding x.

Maddy sighed. "I wish I could have my birthday in New York City surrounded by my two hundred closest friends."

"I don't," I said, scribbling down the problem in my notebook. "Two hundred closest friends implies there are more, and I think Michelle Moriega is just a lonely girl who doesn't know how to deal with her fame. So she makes friends and parties."

"Gosh, Kate." Maddy rolled her eyes. "What do you want to watch instead? The news?" She flicked the remote to the local news station, KCL.

Ted Deffle, the highlighted anchor with the entirely-too-brilliantly-white teeth, was talking. "In other news, yet another victim has been claimed by the man known only as John X." The view switched from somber Ted to a crime scene. "In Chappell today, located in Jefferson County, authorities found the body of Linda Summers, a forty-seven-year-old preschool teacher, outside of a Chappell grocery store."

Maddy grimaced. "That's scary. Jefferson County is just south of us."

"I'm sure it's nothing to be worried about," I said. There are sixty miles of woods between South Woodhaven Falls and Chappell.

"I know. Still …"

Ted continued to talk. "This is the fourth life taken by the still unnamed and unknown killer, currently called John X. Police warn to take extra caution when going in and out of public stores and to keep your doors locked at all times."

"Are your doors locked?" Maddy asked.

I rolled my eyes. "You worry too much." I went back to finding x.

Little did I know x would find me instead.

Another morning, another bowl of Crispix. Only that morning I was up a good thirty minutes too early, thanks to a slobbery face washing by Lolly.

I glared at her as I took my first bite.

Mom saw the look. "Oh good grief, Kate," she said, pulling her two slices of whole wheat toast from the toaster. "Lolly loves you. Don't fault her for that."

Dad was halfway through his power breakfast of eggs, bacon, and a half of a grapefruit. Dad claimed power breakfasts were what made him successful. "I would just like to restate that I was completely against getting a dog in the first place," he said.

Lolly's head drooped.

Dad had the TV going in the background, half listening to KCL and half reading the paper. Mom was lazily thumbing through a book about boundaries or fences or something relational; I was hurriedly eating the Crispix before they got soggy.

"A case that baffled law enforcement and terrorized the public is now officially at an end," the cheerful blonde reporter said on the TV.

All of us looked over.

"John X, the notorious killer who claimed four lives in four counties surrounding St. Louis, was apprehended today in what authorities say was a 'miraculous link.' The one and only witness to John X's third murder, who wishes to remain anonymous, was able to correctly describe John X for the police."

"Wow," Mom said. "That's great!"

"It's about time." Dad nodded.

I slurped up a few more Crispix. They were just starting to get soggy, so I needed to eat fast.

"However," the reporter continued, "a criminal artist who works for a Missouri police department was not the one credited with John X's arrest."

A picture flashed up on the screen and a half-chewed, soggy Crispix fell out of my open mouth and back into my bowl with a tiny splash.

"As we showed you last night on our six-o'clock show, here is the depiction of John X. This is the sketch created by a local South Woodhaven Falls teen, our brightest new criminal sketch artist."

There, very plainly visible in the corner under John X's perfect square chin, was the scrawl that had been perfected over the years. *Kate Carter.*

There was dead silence in my kitchen for all of about ten seconds. Then Mom started screaming, "What? What?"

Dad just looked at me. "Kate Carter. You Kate Carter or a different Kate Carter?"

It was hard to hear him over Mom's screaming. I kept watching the TV, where the drawing I did yesterday in art class was still plastered.

"Authorities say that this drawing of John X is a near photo-quality match of the killer of four. We're hoping to go live to South Woodhaven Falls' very own Kate Carter's house and get a statement from her soon. I'm Candace Olstrom, and this is KCL."

Mom and Dad both stared at me now. The silence was back — this time it lasted a full two minutes.

"How did you know what he looked like?" Dad asked first. Logical question.

"It was a drawing assignment," I said.

"You were assigned to draw a criminal?" Mom gasped.

"Apparently." Detective Masterson's appearance yesterday in art class was more than just to see Miss Yeager's blush, I guessed.

Again, silence.

The quiet was shattered by a knock on the door and Mom whirled to look at Dad. "What if it's John X?"

"He was caught," I said.

"Not now, Kate." Dad said, standing. "Claire, take Kate to the back bedroom and stay there." He was in his protective state. Which, on most dads, was very sweet.

On my dad, it usually involves a gun.

"Dad," I said.

He ignored me and looked at Mom. "Claire, now."

Mom grabbed my elbow and apparently the Crispix were going to win the battle of sogginess this morning. Mom hustled me to the back bedroom, aka the Guest Room. Lolly followed us happily.

"But Dad," I started again as we passed in the hallway.

"Hush," Mom told me as I opened my mouth to protest further. She pushed me down into a sitting position on the bed. "You cannot be too safe. Not mentally, not emotionally, not physically."

I opened my mouth again.

"I mean it. Not a word."

So I sat there on the guest bed. Mom paced the floor, wringing her hands and muttering things like *art teachers* and *lawsuits* under her breath.

A couple of minutes later, Dad walked into the room, a 9mm gun holstered to his hip, escorting a pale and open-mouth-stricken Maddy. "She came to give Kate a ride," Dad said, lightly pushing her toward the bed.

"That's what I was trying to tell you," I said.

Maddy's eyes were the size of snow cones. "What. Is. Going. On."

"Sit," Mom commanded, standing from her spot on the bed. "Neither of you are going to school today."

Maddy gaped at her and then at me. "But what about — ?"

"No excuses," Mom said, staring Maddy down. "Your personal safety is of more concern than a couple of grades."

Maddy just stared at her. "Wait. What happened? Personal safety? Did Mr. Hannigan threaten to put you on the track team again?" She turned to me.

I opened my mouth.

Dad beat me to it. "No, Madison. Kate drew a picture of John X."

Maddy's eyes became snow cone sized again and turned to me. "You what?"

"And it got put on the news," Mom said.

"It's on the news?" Maddy's mouth was still open.

"He got caught, there is no danger," I said.

Dad glared at me, one hand on his 9mm. "I've never trusted that Candace reporter girl. Nobody's voice is really that squeaky. Who knows if he really got arrested?"

"Dad."

He held up a hand. "And I'm going to have more than a word with Miss Yeager or whatever her name is who made you draw a known criminal. What kind of art teacher is she? This isn't *CSI*, these are high school juniors!"

Mom was nodding through Dad's whole sermon. "I am going to talk to her as well. She obviously was not thinking clearly about the damaging effects to the kids' psyches."

"Claire, write a note. We need to contact Pete What's-His-Face and see how we need to go about correcting the school on this."

I sighed. I assumed Dad was talking about Peter Colligher, the attorney they met at the last Parent's Night Out at school. Mr.

Colligher said he specialized in copyright law, so I'm not sure how he was going to help them.

The doorbell rang right as the home phone started ringing. I reached for the handset and my elbow about came out of socket when Mom whacked my hand out of the way and grabbed it herself.

"Dale?" she said, nodding to the entryway and stepping into the hallway with the phone.

"I got the door." Dad nodded and left.

Maddy and I stayed on the bed.

She stared at me. "You drew John X?"

"Well. I didn't mean to."

"How did you know what he looked like?" she asked.

"Detective Masterson told us when he was making Miss Yeager blush," I said.

Maddy's eyes popped even more. "Miss Yeager blushed?"

I nodded.

Mom came back into the room, gripping the phone. "Channel Six wants an interview," she said to me. "I told them by all means, absolutely not."

Dad walked in right then too, carrying a huge bouquet of red roses, followed by a wagging Lolly. "This is from the sheriff's office and Channel Eight has a news crew out there."

Maddy and I were off the couch before he finished talking. We ran to the living room and peered through the cracks in the now-closed drapes.

A news van was parallel parked on the curb in front of our house. About ten people were gathered on the front lawn. Maddy's jet-black Tahoe was in the driveway next to Dad's pickup and my Volvo.

Another news van, with "Channel Two — The News You Can TRUST!" emblazoned on the side drove down the street.

I stepped back and stared at Mom and Dad.

Then at Maddy.

Then at Lolly.

I looked at the TV as the doorbell rang again.

On the screen, there was Candace Olstrom standing on my front porch. "I'm here at the heroic Kate Carter's house, the girl who saved who knows how many lives and brought four victim's souls to justice."

And all I could do was sit down and stare at the TV as Candace continued on about how John X had been terrorizing the four surrounding counties for two months.

I *drew* John X.

I drew John X.

On the one hand, I felt kind of proud that I helped the SWF police in one of the biggest crimes this year, but on the other hand ...

I just knew it. Life was never going to be the same again.

Chapter Four

THE REST OF THE MORNING PASSED IN A BLUR OF THE phone ringing, the doorbell chiming, Maddy's endless questions, and Lolly's head sogging my lap. Dad and Mom both took the day off and Dad was pacing around the house, 9mm still strapped to his waist. He'd allowed us to move to the couch in the living room, but only so he could watch the news and us at the same time.

"So, it was an *assignment*?" Dad asked again, for the fourth time that hour.

I was still watching the front of our house, now being broadcast on Fox News. "Yeah," I said, for the fourth time.

"For drawing class," Dad said.

"Miss Yeager wanted us to see how art as a career could work in everyday life," I said. "I think it was the start of a series."

"A series of criminals?"

"A series of careers." I shook my head.

Dad grumbled something under his breath and continued to pace. Mom was now clicking around on her laptop.

"Kate, listen to this. Criminal sketch artists, or forensic sketch artists, are usually one of the top careers to have mental breakdowns and panic attacks, and of all of the careers available to an artist, they are foremost in needing psychiatric help." She looked up at me, eyes wide. "I do not like this."

Maddy elbowed me in my ribs. "At least you might get a discount," she whispered.

I grinned.

Mom frowned.

Dad noticed my grin, then frowned and launched into lecture-mode. "There is nothing funny about this situation, Kate Carter," he said sternly, one hand on his gun. "This was a dangerous, stupid move for a teacher to have a student make, and you can bet that I'm going to have a very long talk with Miss Yeager or whatever her name is."

I opened my mouth to stick up for Miss Yeager, but the doorbell cut me off.

"Now who is it?" Dad grumbled, sneaking over to the door and peering through the peephole.

We had been instructed that under no circumstances were Maddy or I allowed to look through the curtains, answer the door, look through the peephole, or basically move off the couch unless we were otherwise ordered by Dad.

Dad squinted through the peephole and then growled. "Police guy." He unlocked the door, opened it three inches, reached his arm through, and yanked a uniformed man through the crack before slamming the door shut and locking all the deadbolts again.

"You," Dad barked to the poor guy, who was now trying to smooth his wrinkled and squished uniform. "Start talking."

I still had yet to see the man's face, but then he turned toward me and Maddy sitting on the couch and I waved. "Hi, Detective."

Detective Masterson squinched a half-smile at me and then looked at Dad. "Do you have a permit for that weapon?" he asked.

I was pretty sure this was not the time or the place to ask that question.

Dad seemed to agree with me. He started sputtering so badly that Detective Masterson had to wipe off his cheek.

"My ... my daughter is on Fox News ... and you have the *audacity* to come here and ..." Dad couldn't even finish his sentence, he was so mad. Anytime my very logical, thoughtful father used words like "audacity" and slobbered, I knew it was bad.

"Sir, I'm going to need you to calm down," Detective Masterson said quietly, holding his hands up surrender-style.

Mom was glaring at the detective from the couch. "How do you know my daughter?" she asked icily.

Even Mom was royally ticked. By this point I was starting to realize that the parental units were not going to be cheering me on toward a career in forensic sketching.

If anything, they might be wrapping my hands in a permanent plastic wrap so I'd never be able to draw again.

Detective Masterson turned very slowly away from my dad and faced my mom. "I was present on the day that Kate drew John X."

This did not endear him to my weaponed, spittle-encrusted father. "You encouraged this?" he demanded.

"Sir, ma'am," the detective said, looking at both my parents. "Your daughter has supreme talent in this field and I believe that it was no accident that she was instrumental in helping us apprehend John X."

Maddy elbowed me again when Detective Masterson said "supreme talent."

I was suddenly very hungry for pizza.

Very hungry and very flattered. I peeked over at my dad to see how he was taking this, considering the Master Plan was for me to follow in his mathematical, engineering footsteps.

He was still sputtering.

"Now, all that being said, I do need to formally apologize for both having Kate draw John X and for the way the sketch was leaked to the press. When Kate's art teacher came to us to have us discuss the career of criminal sketching, she and I both thought it could be beneficial for the students to attempt a sketch of a known criminal." Detective Masterson winced. "I didn't, however, anticipate your daughter having such a natural talent. Nor did I anticipate that the sketches would be taken off my desk and shown to the witness who saw John X." He nodded at me. "But it was no accident."

Mom was still glaring at the detective. "You believe in fate," she said.

"No, ma'am. I believe that God orchestrated this."

Oh, now this was just getting better all the time. I felt my eyes widen. Dad tolerated Mom's attempts to get this family to be more spiritual, but I was imagining that mixing religiosity with his daughter's safety was not a smart move for the detective.

Even though we were faithfully in the church pew every year at Christmas thanks to my mother, who wanted us to experience a "spiritual" side of life, Dad did not go willingly. If anything, he was dragged there purely from the desire to sleep in his bed that night instead of on the couch. And Mom, who pretended to listen intently, was not that interested in Christianity.

"It's just good to keep our names on the list," she would tell me. "Plus, goodness knows you and your father need something to balance your logical bones."

I doubt she'd still call me logical at this moment.

"God?" Dad gasped out the word. I was waiting for "oh, kill me now" to follow his exclamation, but the doorbell rang yet again, saving the detective from a nice verbal lashing.

Dad peered again through the peephole. "More of you," he announced to Detective Masterson.

The detective nodded. "We are going to take Kate to the police station."

Dad started sputtering again, and this time Mom joined him.

Detective Masterson quickly hurried up and finished his thought. "We need to question her, and we also want to be mindful of her safety right now. As well as all of your safety." He looked at Maddy.

Maddy leaned back against the couch. "I wonder if I'll still have to take that geography exam," she said quietly.

"We will be certain to arrange things with the school," the detective said, obviously overhearing Maddy.

"Absolutely not," Dad finally got out.

"But Mr. Carter, my geography exam counts for a third of my final grade," Maddy protested.

Dad didn't even spare her a glance. "We are not going down to the police station."

"Sir," Detective Masterson said.

"Dad," I said.

"Dale," Mom said.

"You already had my daughter draw a murderer. What could you possibly need her to do now? Draw a gang leader? A drug lord? The guy who piloted the plane in *Con Air*?" Dad was ranting now.

And Dad didn't even like that movie. He said that no guy with Nicolas Cage's hairstyle would have ever ended up with a woman who looked like his wife.

I have to admit, I had to agree. And Mom just told us to hush because she had a thing for Nicolas Cage — scraggly, long hair or not.

Maddy elbowed me yet again. "What is *Con Air*?" she whispered.

"Sir, this really is the best option," the detective said calmly. The doorbell rang again. "Actually, it's the only option. Our primary responsibility now is to keep you and your family safe. And we only want to question Kate, not hire her." When Dad didn't budge, Detective Masterson nodded. "You really have no other choice, sir."

"Dale," Mom said. "We need to go."

Dad shook his head and walked down the hallway. We all just looked at each other for the next thirty seconds. Was he on his way to get the rest of his arsenal? Was he calling Pete What's-His-Name?

Dad came back with a coat a minute later. "Kate, what are you doing?" he barked. "Get your coat and shoes. We're going with Detective Masterson or whatever he calls himself."

I ran down the hall to my room and found my Chuck Taylors. I glanced in the mirror as I was about to leave. I never thought I'd be on TV, and I especially never thought I'd be on TV while wearing my least attractive pair of jeans. They were ripped on the right knee and shredded around the hemlines because I'm short and most of my pants aren't.

I shrugged and grabbed my favorite red hoodie jacket.

Maddy was waiting with my parents and Detective Masterson by the front door. She was still wearing her backpack and a wide-eyed expression.

"We are going to be on TV!" she hissed in my ear when I joined them.

"I know," I whispered back.

"I didn't curl my hair very well today," she moaned.

"Okay," the detective said. "Here's what will happen. We will surround you and try to get you into the police vehicles with minimum amount of camera exposure. So stay together, and stay close to us."

He opened the door and nodded to a bunch of uniformed guys on my front porch.

Immediately, we were all surrounded and shoved en masse toward a couple of police cars parked right smack in the middle of my father's front lawn. Yet another occurrence that had him bristling.

Mom and Dad were stuck in the back of one police car, and Maddy and I were put into the other one. Meanwhile, there were cameras and flashes and microphones and people screaming, "Kate! Kate! How did you know what John X looked like? What is it like being the town heroine? Kate!"

I didn't get a chance to even answer them because the door was slammed the second my feet were out of the way.

Chapter Five

DETECTIVE MASTERSON RODE IN THE PASSENGER SEAT and another policeman drove.

"Girls, this is Officer Walker," he said.

"I guess that's fitting," Maddy whispered to me as we drove off the curb, leaving some nice tire marks there for my dad to stress over. "You know, the whole Walker name and him being a ranger and all."

"But he's an officer," I said. "And I'm pretty sure he's not from Texas."

"Yeah, but he's still into the whole keeping-the-law, protecting-people bit. You never know, maybe that guy has almost been run over by an unmanned plane before."

"Walker was almost run over by an unmanned plane?" I asked.

She shrugged. "I don't know. I usually watch E!"

The police station was only three miles from my house, so it didn't take too long to get there. There were reporters there too, though, so once again we got surrounded and hustled inside while people were yelling at me and waving cameras in my face.

Once we got inside, there was a huge room, filled with tons of cubicles.

I'd never been to prison, but I kind of imagined it would look more like Alcatraz than the set from *The Office*.

Mom and Dad joined us in the entrance of the big room, and

Detective Masterson waved for us to follow him down one of the outside aisles and into a small room that was off to the side.

There was a table, six chairs, and a pitcher of water in there.

"Wow, is this where you interrogate criminals?" Maddy asked the detective, her voice all hushed for the souls gone before us.

"We have concentrated staff meetings here," Detective Masterson said, nodding to the chairs.

I guess there was no need for the hushed voice.

Right then a tall, heavy, older-looking guy wearing a business suit walked in and closed the door behind him.

"Please, have a seat," he told us and we all sat. Mom and Dad sat on either side of me, and Maddy and Detective Masterson sat next to the older guy across the table from us.

"I'm Gene Slalom, the deputy chief of police here in South Woodhaven Falls," he said, all deep and booming voiced. He didn't sound at all like I thought deputies sounded. But maybe that was because my entire basis for deputies was founded on Barney Fife from *The Andy Griffith Show*.

We all nodded.

"That's Kate," Detective Masterson said, pointing to me.

"Ah." Deputy Slalom said, looking at me without smiling. "Hello, Kate."

"Hello, Deputy Slalom."

Awkward silence. I almost wanted to ask if he skied or not, considering his name, but I held my tongue. They brought me here, they can talk.

"Nice conference room," Maddy said.

Or Maddy could talk.

"Thank you." Deputy Slalom nodded at Maddy. "We recently updated the paint. It used to have wallpaper."

I looked over at the neutral tan color while Maddy smiled. "Good choice. Wallpaper is very out of style."

She would know.

He nodded again and looked away from Maddy. "Kate, Mr.

and Mrs. Carter, we brought you here because Kate has done her city, her state, and her country a service that can never be repaid."

"What kind of danger is my daughter in?" Dad asked.

"Do you have any idea what this type of situation will do to a young girl's psyche?" Mom said at the same time.

Deputy Slalom held up both of his hands. "Trust me, we will get to all of your questions." He leaned across the table and looked at me. "But first, Kate Carter, I wanted to extend a hand of thanks."

He reached across the table to shake my hand, and I have to admit, I've never been given a hand of thanks before.

"Thanks," I said.

"No. Thank you."

"Oh. Well. You're welcome."

Handshake dispensed with, he turned to my parents. "Okay. Danger. Kate is in a significant amount of danger. John X was not believed to have any accomplices, but then we won't know for sure until we are able to extensively question him, and we have been unable to do so for the past twelve hours."

Dad glared at Detective Masterson.

"That being said, we will have around-the-clock protection for Kate. She will take one of my officers to school with her and we will also have at least one, if not two, officers in your home night and day."

"Two," Dad said. "I don't want even the chance of something happening."

"Understandable, sir. And while this is a regrettable situation to be in, it is also one that will bring a tremendous amount of relief to many people in this state, you do realize. Your daughter is a hero."

"Heroine," Maddy corrected.

"What about *her* mental state?" Mom asked. "You do realize how much stress this puts her under, don't you?"

It is definitely a huge pet peeve of mine when people talk about me in front of me like I'm not even there.

"We do realize," the deputy said. "And we have a staff psychiatrist that has supervised many a witness case and will be working with Kate as well."

I raised my hand. "But I can still go to school?" We were covering how to multiply and divide fractions in algebra. And knowing my dad's teaching skills, I'd rather learn from my algebra teacher than Dad.

"Yes, you can still go to school." He raised a hand to cut off my parents' immediate rebuttal. "Accompanied by an officer, of course."

A lady knocked on the door and then opened it, sticking her head in. "Sorry to interrupt, sir, but the mayor is here and wants to meet Kate."

Deputy Slalom winced slightly and then nodded. "Send him in."

A minute later, in walked Arnold Walinski, who was arguably the biggest schmoozer you could ever meet. I was pretty sure he prided himself on having the most handshakes of any mayor in Missouri — and coming from such a small town, that said a lot.

"Kate Carter," he said warmly to Maddy.

She pointed to me and Arnold didn't even skip a beat. "So nice to meet the girl who saved our town from disaster!"

And here I thought that disasters were typically made up of those mudslides that our gym teacher liked to tell us about.

"Hi, Mayor," I said, shaking his outstretched hand. "I don't think I saved our town from anything. Was John X even around South Woodhaven Falls?"

Detective Masterson shook his head. "Ballwin," he said, naming one of the neighboring suburbs.

"Regardless," Arnold said. "Kate, it would be my honor and privilege to have you and your family join me and my wife for dinner at the mayor's house Saturday night." He was grinning in a way that I thought was supposed to be welcoming, but it ended up just looking toothy and cheesy.

And I was now going to refer to my house as "the Carter's house."

"Um," I said, looking at Mom.

She shrugged. "Sure," she said after looking over her shoulder at Dad, who nodded rather stiffly. Dad was not one for hobnobbing with politicians. He said they got annoying and that while most of them could talk circles around a band of turkeys, they couldn't hold one straightforward conversation to save their lives.

I wasn't sure that turkeys ran together in bands, but whatever.

"Fabulous, fabulous!" Arnold started crooning. "I'll not interrupt your conversation with these fine gentlemen any longer. See you this weekend, Kate and family."

He left whistling.

Deputy Slalom waited until the door was closed and latched before he started up again. "Where was I? Oh yes. School." He nodded to me. "You will take an officer to school with you tomorrow."

"Are you sure it's safe for her to be returning to school so soon?" Mom asked.

"She'll be fine with Officer Kirkpatrick." The deputy nodded to Detective Masterson. "And if the need comes up, I can send Detective Masterson as well, just to monitor the situation."

Judging by the slight redness to his cheeks, I was thinking that Miss Yeager was contributing more toward the detective's presence at school than my imminent danger.

"I ... I guess if you think it's safe ..." Mom stumbled.

Dad was resorting to silence. Meaning he didn't agree.

"Wonderful," Deputy Slalom said. "Now, if you and Maddy could wait outside, we have some questions we need to ask Kate alone. Margo out there can get you some refreshments."

My parents got up and left, looking sadly at me as they walked out the door. Maddy whispered, "Remember everything!" and then followed them out.

And then it was just me with the two policemen.

"Kate," Deputy Slalom started. He had his hands woven together and sitting on the table. Detective Masterson looked more at ease, lounging back in his chair.

"Yes?"

"Kent here has told me that you are a remarkable artist," Deputy Slalom said, angling his head toward the detective.

Kent. Awkward name, no offense to the detective.

I shrugged. I don't take compliments well. Mom said that's a reflection of a lack of self-confidence and one of the top three signs of a loner, but I said it's just because I don't get them too frequently. Practice makes perfect. I'm barely over five feet tall. There's not much here to compliment.

Which is when Dad told me that I had nice earlobes.

"I have to admit, when Miss Yeager came to us and asked if we could help explain the forensic sketch artist career field to a bunch of high schoolers, I was less than enthusiastic," Deputy Slalom said. "I guess we can see who was wrong. Anyway, I have something I want to ask you, but I don't want an answer today. Actually, I don't want an answer until all this insanity with John X is over and done with."

I was trying not to cringe in my chair, waiting for the word *babysitter.* I wasn't sure what it was with adults, but I tend to attract potential babysitting jobs like Lindsay Lohan attracts miniskirts.

I was not a babysitter. I didn't like kids. I did not like the way they smelled or the way they had some weird fascination with Dora. Any show that makes little kids think it's perfectly normal to talk to and interact with a television set was breeding future clients for my mother, if you ask me.

I waited for Deputy Slalom to finish his thought.

He leaned across the desk. "Kate, you are a very nonthreatening person."

"Please don't tell my father that." He would send me back to that self-defense class again.

"You're very nice, you seem to listen before you speak," the deputy continued. "And I already mentioned the artistic talent."

Maybe he wanted me to draw pictures of his kids.

"Kate, I'd like you to consider joining the police force as a junior member."

I just blinked at him.

"I really feel like we need a female forensic sketch artist and witnesses need someone who is nonthreatening to talk to, especially women and children."

I opened my mouth to protest, and he held up his hand.

"I told you to think on it, Kate. It's just a thought. Though, I think it's a good thought, and Kent here agrees with me."

I did not know why hearing the word *Kent* kept throwing me off.

The deputy smiled very briefly and very tiredly at me. "Thanks again, Kate."

I nodded.

We all stood, and Detective Masterson opened the door for us. Outside, there was a redheaded police officer talking with my parents.

"This is Officer Kirkpatrick," the deputy said. "Get used to him, he'll be around."

"Hello, Kate," the officer said. He couldn't have been more than about twenty-five, and he was tall and kind of on the skinny side.

He didn't look very menacing. I think my dad was thinking the same thing as he sized him up.

"Hi," I said. "So you are following me around now."

He did one of those little smiles that was half friendly, half pained. I guess I couldn't blame him, considering it did mean going back to high school for him.

"We'll take you guys back home. If anyone requests an interview, please refuse it for the time being. And Kate, you will probably receive a lot of offers for various things ... just turn them all down," Detective Masterson said. "Shall we?" He motioned to the door.

We got back home and it was just me, Mom, Dad, Maddy, Lolly, and Officer Kirkpatrick.

And it was silent.

Mom looked exhausted and went into the kitchen. I could sense a vanilla-laced bath in her near future. Dad was still strapped to his gun and followed Mom into the kitchen. Maddy sat on the couch and reached for the remote.

Officer Kirkpatrick stood in the doorway, pensively. And I had to wonder how much of the pensiveness was because Lolly wouldn't stop smelling the guy.

"Lolly. Cut it out," I said, patting my leg.

She didn't cut it out.

"Lolly."

Maddy whistled, not taking her eyes off the TV. "Lolly, cheese!" she yelled.

Lolly immediately bolted toward Maddy on the couch.

"Good girl, good girl," Maddy crooned to her.

"Where's the cheese?" I asked. "You can't promise something and not give it to her then. Now she won't come the next time."

Lolly, depressed because of the lack of cheese, slumped in front of the couch in a dog heap.

"Hey, Officer Kirkpatrick," Maddy said, ignoring me, angling her head toward him, but waiting for the story about some star's new love interest to end before she moved her eyes.

"Yes, Madison?"

"What's your first name?"

Officer Kirkpatrick squinted at her. "Darrell."

Now I looked at him. I was not sure how a couple could look at a scrawny little redheaded baby and name him Darrell. Judging from Maddy's expression, she agreed.

"Your name is really Darrell?" I asked.

"It's a family name. My great-uncle's name is Darrell."

"Well, my great-aunt's name is Olga and my parents were kind enough to forgo family tradition," Maddy said, going back to Ryan Seacrest's rundown of all the top "news."

Seriously, since when did seeing Sienna Miller sans makeup on her way to the gym become news?

Darrell Kirkpatrick shrugged at me. "He didn't have any kids, and my dad was always pretty attached to him."

I asked, "So you go by Darrell?"

"I go by DJ. My middle name is Jefferson."

I wanted to say that was a big name for a little guy, but for some reason, I didn't think our friendly officer would like that. And considering he was going to be following me around for the foreseeable future, I wanted to be on his good side.

"So, should I call you Officer Kirkpatrick or DJ?" I asked.

He thought about it. "DJ. At school, I'm going to be dressed in plain clothes."

School.

I really needed to study for my test tomorrow. I nodded. "Well, it's time for me to get to studying."

Madison looked at the still-closed blinds on the front windows. "I don't think I'm going to go home until my parents will be there," she said. "If it's okay with you, I'm going to stay here and watch TV."

"Fine with me."

I went to my room and shut the door. It was the first time all day I had been alone.

I took a deep breath and closed my eyes.

Which is when someone knocked.

"Yes?" I yelled, quietness shattered.

"It's DJ. You need to leave your door open, Kate."

I opened it and looked at him. "How am I supposed to use the bathroom or take a shower or get dressed?"

He nodded. "The bathroom doesn't have any windows. You can shut the door when you are in there. But not in your room."

He smiled a friendly smile and then moved to the hallway where he could see almost all of the house.

I was going to have to have a very serious talk with Miss Yeager tomorrow.

Chapter Six

FRIDAY MORNING. APPROXIMATELY FIFTEEN MINUTES before the bell was scheduled to ring.

School looked normal enough. I was peering out the windows of the unmarked police car that DJ had driven me to school in. Apparently, me driving by myself was a definite no. DJ did swap the uniform with a pair of jeans and a Polo shirt though.

Still. So much for all the privileges that came with that hard-earned driver's license.

DJ, who looked as refreshed as a man could look after sleeping on an air mattress in the hallway of my house, was looking out the window too. Another policeman, Officer Colton, came at night as well, only he stayed awake so DJ could sleep.

"Let me get out first and you follow. Your first class is drawing. You are to be no more than five feet away from me at any given moment. Understood?"

I wondered if this is what the daughters of the president had to go through and I immediately was overcome with despair for them. Dad always said that pity is pointless. Mom said it's only pointless if we don't do something to help.

Aside from kidnapping the first daughters and showing them what life outside of a security detail was like, which I imagined was a federal crime to the highest degree, I couldn't think of a way to help them.

So I stopped pitying them and glared at DJ instead.

"Hey," he said, holding his hands up. "I didn't draw John X."

"I didn't mean to."

Good thing art was first. Miss Yeager and I were about to have it out.

DJ got out of the car and I followed him as instructed. What I didn't expect was that all the news crews that had been parked outside my house for half the night would be at SWF High.

"Kate! Kate!" one lady yelled incessantly at me as DJ hustled me into the school.

I would think there must be more exciting news in South Woodhaven Falls, but surely there was not. One of the perks and apparently curses of living in a small town.

I remembered when Dusty McSweeny, the local grocer, put up the very first "Handicapped Parking Only" sign in all of South Woodhaven Falls in front of his store. That was the only news we got for the next three nights. People were getting their picture beside it and making bad jokes about it like, "Hey, did you see the new sign outside of McSweeny's? It's pretty handy!"

Suddenly, I found myself wishing for another natural "disaster" like the Great Tornado of 1993 that took out a woman's leaning storage shed and knocked over a couple of other people's grills. That story lasted on the local news for about three weeks.

DJ and I made it inside, barely, and then the real chaos started.

"Hey, it's Kate Carter!" one guy I'd never seen before in my life shouted.

"Kate Carter?" another girl I did not know repeated.

"Kate Carter?"

"Kate Carter!"

Suddenly, my name was being repeated so consistently and on such a good beat that I was waiting for the music to start and my personhood to be sung about like what happens in *High School Musical*. DJ kept pushing me toward my locker.

"Wow, that was really brave," one guy said as we passed him.

He was actually kind of cute, so I wouldn't have minded talking to him, but DJ didn't seem to care. It was all for the better, anyway. We already know my history with guys.

I grabbed my pencils and sketchpad from my locker and then heard another rousing chorus of "Kate Carter!" and "Wow, that was amazing what you did!" as I was rounded into art class.

Considering my history of tardiness, I wasn't even sure what to expect as I pushed open the classroom door at ten minutes until class time. Miss Yeager was busy writing instructions on the board, and no one else was there yet.

She turned when she heard the door close and at first she smiled. "Kate!" she said excitedly. Then I guess she noticed the man behind me and the firm set to my jawline.

"How are you?" she asked all hesitantly, putting the dry erase marker down and walking over slowly.

"Well," I started, ready to unload on her.

Which of course is when Silent Justin walked in. I almost growled in frustration. I couldn't lambaste Miss Yeager in front of a classmate. It's like the highest form of insult to get mad at an authority figure in front of her subordinates.

Or so I thought. My knowledge of authority and subordinates is completely from movies like *The Guardian* and *Remember the Titans*. Which was about the only thing I took from those movies, other than a fear of boating or swimming in the ocean.

"Good morning, Justin," Miss Yeager said to my classmate. She got a grunt of recognition before turning back to me.

"Miss Yeager," I said, carefully, keeping one eye on Justin as he started arranging his pencils on our table. "Were you aware that we were sketching a nationally known and state-feared criminal when you had me complete the last assignment?"

Miss Yeager looked at me and then at DJ.

"Kate," she started.

"Did you know we were sketching John X?"

She took a deep breath. "No, for the record, I did not know it was John X. I knew it was a man who had committed a crime and hadn't been caught, but I was not aware it was him."

Which placed the blame squarely on the good Detective Masterson's shoulders.

"I see," I said. I went to my table and sat down.

"Kate," Miss Yeager said again, apology reigning in her tone.

"Miss Yeager, I can barely even go to the bathroom by myself now. My dad's constantly got his 9mm strapped to his chest, my mom is on the verge of a mental breakdown, and I'm constantly shadowed by *him*." I jerked my thumb toward DJ.

He smiled and waved at Miss Yeager. "Officer Kirkpatrick. Pleased to meet you."

"Likewise." She was smiling back at him.

I really hoped I wasn't interrupting the moment. Oh wait, yes I did.

"Seriously, you guys?"

"Okay, okay," Miss Yeager said, coming over and putting a hand on my shoulder. "Listen, Kate, I'm very sorry about the sketching assignment. But, if it makes you feel better and it should, you are the person to thank for protecting our state from a very dangerous man. And you wouldn't have gotten that opportunity without the detective providing you with that assignment."

Justin was sitting directly to my left, and he made a tiny noise in the back of his throat like he agreed.

That sent me over the edge. "Look, instead of grunting like a caveman, why don't you just speak? We all know you can. Gosh!"

"Kate Carter!" Miss Yeager exclaimed, only it wasn't in the adoring way that everyone outside in the halls was proclaiming it.

"Sorry," I mumbled. I rubbed my head. I hadn't even taken a good shower this morning — I was so weirded out by the fact that DJ was standing in the hall waiting for me. I could feel the start of several zits along my hairline.

Fabulous.

I held my head for a few seconds and then looked over at Justin, who was flipping through his sketchbook. "Sorry," I said.

He nodded.

Wordlessly, of course.

Miss Yeager sighed. "Listen, Kate, I understand that you've been through a lot of emotions in the last twenty-four hours. In fact, I really wasn't even anticipating you being here today at all."

"I've got a geography exam."

She smiled at me. "I think Mr. Walsh might have let you take it later, all things considered."

I just blinked at her. If I didn't come to school, what would I do? Sit on the couch with DJ and Lolly and watch E! reruns?

All last night, I dreamt about some shadowy figure sitting in a jail cell and carving *Get Kate Carter* over his cell door like the poor man in *The Count of Monte Cristo*. Only that man was carving the name of the woman he loved.

I was fairly sure that John X did not harbor feelings of affection of any kind toward me. Even though my dad said that prison these days was better than the outside world, because apparently they get cable, no taxes, basketball games, and pot roast. Dad said that if he weren't an upstanding citizen, he would have hoped to get into prison years ago.

Part of me thought my dad was just kidding because I've seen some of those documentaries on the Discovery Channel about life in the slammer. I've never seen anyone playing basketball in the yard. All the clips they ever show are the ones where the guards were breaking up one of the daily fights with tear gas and bean bag guns.

No, it was better to be at school. At school, I have to concentrate on art and math and what the population in the capital of Brazil was. At home, I would be researching prison and worrying.

"I'm fine," I said, pretty much lying through my teeth, but trying to look calm as I wove my fingers together and set my hands on top of my sketchbook.

Miss Yeager didn't look like she believed me, but she nodded. "Fine."

She walked back to the board, DJ moved to the back corner of the class, and the bell buzzed once as a flood of bodies came through the door.

I felt Justin looking at me, but when I looked over at him, he snapped his head around so fast I heard his neck pop.

Then again, he wasn't the only one looking. Everyone was craning their heads as they sat down, gawking at me and whispering.

I will never stare at babies in McSweeny's Market whose mothers dress them in horrendous clothing again. I know now what it feels like.

"Okay, everyone, stop staring at Kate," Miss Yeager said finally, as the second bell rang.

Allison Northing dropped into her chair beside me right as the bell finished. "Oh my gosh, Kate, I cannot *believe* you are here today!" she tried to whisper but didn't really succeed. "Oh wow, did you know who we were drawing? Did you get like an award or something? Holy cow, you should *totally* hang it in your locker!"

"Today, we are going to continue with our discussions on how to use art in the career world," Miss Yeager started and, thankfully, Allison quieted.

I tried to focus on what Miss Yeager was saying, but honestly, the word *career* just reminded me of Deputy Slalom's job offer yesterday.

Now, granted, I had told Mom and Dad that I wanted to look into getting a job over the summer. Something with casual work attire, nice hourly pay, and good benefits. I was thinking about maybe working at Kelly's Creamery and serving ice cream. For every ten cones you sold, you got one free.

That sounded like good benefits to me.

Dad wanted me to consider working at the local hardware store. I figured he wanted some discounts for when he finally built that shed he'd been talking about building for years.

I didn't like the smell of sawdust, however, and the hardware store always smelled of sawdust and wood glue. Which also made me worry a little bit about the architectural integrity of the store.

But working as a forensic sketch artist? With the police?

I was willing to bet there was no free ice cream with that job.

"… makes it one of the best choices for an art major's career," Miss Yeager said, and I shook my head slightly, trying to bring myself back to the present.

I raised my hand.

"Yes, Kate?"

"I'm sorry. What's one of the best choices for an art major's career?" I asked, feeling dumb but not wanting to miss what she was talking about. Justin wouldn't have answered me if I'd asked him and Allison doesn't know the meaning of whispering.

Miss Yeager smiled faintly at me. "Freelance artistry," she said. She looked at the class. "I have several friends who make a very good living contracting out with people to design their restaurant menus, drawing the winter art you see on store windows, and painting creative pieces on people's walls. You have to be willing to keep very unusual hours and have very good self-marketing skills, but it can be a great line of work."

She told us that we would now spend the rest of class designing a menu. "I want you to use your creative brains and come up with a restaurant, a good description of the kind of food they serve, and a sample menu for me. I need it in color and finished on my desk by Monday morning. Don't worry about putting prices on there."

She walked around handing out huge sheets of paper that had been pre-folded into a menu with three sections.

Allison immediately started working on hers. She'd only had her paper for seventeen seconds before *Allison's Awesome Appetizer House* was written across the top of the front page.

Justin was lightly sketching a few lines here and there, making what looked like a vine wrapping around the edges of the menu. I was willing to bet his was going to be an Italian restaurant.

Everyone around me was working and sketching. I stared at my blank piece of paper.

All I could think about was John X whiling away time in prison by cutting my name into the rubber sole of his shoelace-less shoes, listening to a basketball game outside his window while the smell of pot roast wafted down the barred hallway.

"Kate?" Miss Yeager said softly.

I jerked up. "Oh. Yes?"

She just smiled one of those sad, sympathetic smiles at me. "You don't have to be here," she said.

I nodded. "Yes, I do." I picked up my pencil.

I worked quickly and I worked hard. By the time class was over, I had a halfway decent menu about halfway done.

Granted, it was for a restaurant called *Jailbird's* and the main thing they served was pot roast, but it was done very tastefully in an art-deco design.

The bell rang and everyone stuffed their pencils, menus, and sketchpads into their backpacks. "Have a great weekend everyone, see you on Monday!" Miss Yeager yelled over the chaos.

DJ waited for me while I gathered up my supplies. "So," he said as I shrugged on my backpack. "Jailbird's?"

"DJ," I said, walking into the loud hallway and trying to ignore yet another chorus of "Kate Carter! Kate Carter? Kate Carter!"

"Yes, Kate?"

"Do they serve pot roast in prison?"

Chapter Seven

SOMEHOW, I GOT THROUGH THE REST OF THE DAY WITH minimal visions of John X in his cell and only hearing my name shouted another eighty-seven times. Maddy caught me in the hall right before lunch and warned me to just give her my lunch money and she'd meet me by her car to eat it.

So Maddy, DJ, and I ate school cafeteria lunches in her shiny, black Tahoe. I don't believe I've ever eaten something that disgusting in something so nice. Our cafeteria excels in only two lunches — pizza and soft tacos with Spanish rice.

Today's lunch was cold chicken nuggets and congealed macaroni and cheese.

Needless to say, both DJ and I were starving when we got home.

Mom, still on the verge of a nervous breakdown, apparently cancelled her afternoon appointments so she could worry over me when I got home.

"Kate!" she cried as soon as I walked in the door.

"Hi, Mom," I said as she grabbed me into one of those almost-painful hugs, it was so tight.

"Oh, Kate, I worried about you all day today. School was uneventful? People were kind to you? The pressure wasn't too hard to take?"

"I think I passed my geography test," I told her.

She looked up at DJ, who nodded. "I think she handled it just fine, ma'am."

Mom stopped crushing me to her chest, but kept one hand on my shoulder. "I made cookies."

"Great," I said, trying to muster up some enthusiasm. Cookies, to my mom, usually involved some form of natural sweetener that isn't called sugar. And while I thought that sugar was the only natural sweetener, it is not.

Two weeks ago, she'd made a batch of honey and wheat germ cookies. No refined sugar, no white flour.

"You are supposed to dip them into a nice, hot cup of tea," Mom said to me and Dad when she served them.

Dad had made a face and then dunked his "cookie" into the tea and shoved the whole thing in his mouth. "Mm!" he managed and then got up from the table.

The cookie was rock solid. I think you had to dunk it in the tea to help it soften enough for your temporomandibular joint to work.

So I wasn't too excited when Mom mentioned cookies. This meant more acting and after seven hours of acting like I was fine and focused at school, I was ready to just have some alone time.

And by alone time, I meant me in my bedroom with the door open while DJ took his post in the hallway.

"Chocolate chip." Mom nodded.

My head snapped up so fast, I nearly bit my tongue. "You made chocolate chip cookies?" I gasped.

I had to see it to believe it. I went into the kitchen and lo and behold, there on the counter were dozens of cookies dotted with dark chocolate chips.

DJ and Mom followed me. "It's not like I never make chocolate chip cookies," Mom was telling DJ.

I was pretty sure that the last time she made them, I was still learning the Pledge of Allegiance.

"With real sugar?" I asked, dubiously sniffing a cookie.

"Yes," Mom said.

Then I rethought my question. "I mean, with fake sugar?"

She sighed. "Just eat the cookie, Kate."

I took a bite. And it was definitely not a chocolate chip cookie.

But I pulled on my theater skills and managed to swallow it. Whatever was in the cookie was acting like a vacuum on my saliva. I could barely get the last of it down, my mouth was so dry. "You did use real sugar," I said after downing a glass of water.

"Yep. This one is made from the leaves of the stevia plant," Mom said proudly. "And that's whole wheat flour, carob chips, and don't tell your father, but I added some whey protein powder to give them a little nutritional boost."

DJ was staring at the cookies like they were on the same playing field as our lunch today.

So much for starving. "I won't tell Dad," I said and then grabbed my backpack and went to my room.

My room was possibly my favorite place in this house. I painted it a deep chocolate color last year, and I'd slowly been adding different colors and textures in my accessories to provide visual depth and interest. My bedspread was a rich ruby red, I'd hung a few shelves that were a creamy color, and I was trying to locate some textured pillows for my bed.

I plopped my backpack by my desk and climbed up on the bed, dragging my sketchpad, pencils, and half-finished menu over.

The menu was due on Monday, and since art was my favorite subject, I always tried to do that homework first.

I heard the TV turn on in the living room. "In South Woodhaven Falls, Missouri, yesterday, a high school junior was directly related to the arrest of famed murderer, John X . . ."

"Oh my gosh!" I heard Mom say. "Kate, get in here! Katie Couric is talking about you!"

I walked into the living room, and DJ followed me. There was Katie Couric and there was my yearbook picture suspended in the air next to her.

I hated that picture. Of all the ones they had to use, they had to pick one that made me look like a squinty third grader.

Katie Couric started retelling the now-infamous story, and the phone rang. Mom answered it and then passed it to me.

"Did you know that you're on Katie Couric?"

It was Maddy.

"I'm watching it right now."

"Did you see the picture they used?"

I sighed. "Maddy, I'm watching it right now."

"I wish they'd come to me for a picture. I would have at least given them the one of us at the zoo last summer."

I knew exactly which picture she was talking about and she was right, that was a lot cuter.

"Since when do you watch the news, Maddy?"

"Since never. I was flipping through the channels, and I saw you squinting at me. Hey, if Ryan Seacrest decides to interview you, will you let me go with you? I'll give them the cute picture of you."

I just shook my head at the TV, which was now showing a picture of the jailed John X. He didn't look too happy in his mug shot, and a lone skittle of fear raced up my spinal column.

"Sure, Maddy. Sure."

Mom called me in for dinner at 5:37, yet another sign that not all was well in our house. Dad had just gotten home, and DJ was standing guard in the living room.

"How was school?" Dad asked, the first normal question I'd gotten all day.

I opened my mouth to respond.

"Oh, and I looked into getting you in some self-defense and gun handling classes. You're too young to carry a concealed weapon, but your self-defense class starts on Tuesday night at seven. You and your mother are both signed up to go."

So, it started out normal.

I nodded. "Okay." At this point, it was better not to argue.

We went into the kitchen, and Mom guilted DJ into sitting in Mike's empty chair. "I made enough for you to eat, so if you don't, I'm going to be very hurt," Mom said, putting a platter of what looked like salmon on the table.

"Okay, ma'am. If you say so."

Mom may not be able to do the sweet stuff well, but she usually made awesome dinners. The salmon smelled so good, and we all sat at the table, drooling.

Lolly was lounging on the floor, waiting for someone to drop a bite.

As was custom, Mom held out her hands and Dad made a gruffly noise in the back of his throat.

"Bless the food. Amen," he muttered, barely bothering to close his eyes.

Well. Some things hadn't changed.

Dad, DJ, and I all dug into our salmon, but Mom was more reluctant. I could tell she was trying to decide if she should say something or not.

"Guys?" she said, finally, putting her unused fork down. "We are going to church this Sunday."

Everyone just kind of stared at her in a chewing silence.

"What?" Dad said.

"Why?" I asked.

"Sounds like a plan." DJ nodded. "Great salmon, Mrs. Carter."

Mom said thank you to DJ and then looked at me and my dad. "Because it has been a long time since we were there, and I just feel like we need all the help we can get right now."

She picked up her fork and took a bite of salmon. I looked across the table at Dad, who shrugged and started on his rice.

So it looked like I wasn't going to be sleeping in on Sunday.

"What did you do in school today?" Dad asked me.

"I took a geography exam."

"Did you pass it?"

"Yes, sir."

Dad nodded, content.

A few minutes of quiet chewing took place. Lolly stirred under the table, reminding us that she was still there.

"I talked to Mike today," Mom said, and both Dad and I immediately snapped to attention.

"Is he okay?" I asked.

"Did he total his car or something?" Dad said.

Mom sent us both a glare. "He's fine."

"How's his car, though?" Dad asked.

"He's fine, his car is fine, his grades are fine, and he was just calling because he heard about Kate on the radio this morning, and he wanted to know if it was our Kate or a different one."

My brother moved out to go to college in California almost three years ago. In that time, he had only made it home for the two Christmas breaks he had and opted to stay out there for both Thanksgivings.

As for me, I hadn't talked to him on the phone the entire time he'd been gone. There's five years and personality issues between us — his personality issues, not mine.

So the fact that he called of his own free will was something of a miracle. I think that Mom tried to call him about once a week, but she only ended up getting through to him about once a month.

Mom would never admit to it, but I did see her crying a little last month when she once again got my brother's voicemail.

It made me mad at Mike. The woman went through thirty-two hours of labor and eighteen years of feeding and caring for him. You'd think he could spare a few minutes to talk to his mother on the phone.

Dad always said that an engineering degree was one of the toughest degrees out there, and we should just let Mike study.

I thought it was just another excuse for my brother.

"So, he's doing okay?" I asked. Mad or not, Mike was still my brother.

Mom nodded. "He only had a minute to talk, but he said he's doing good. Said classes are hard, but the weather is nice."

So, pretty much, he got through the perfunctory stuff and then hung up.

I shook my head slightly and kept working on my salmon and rice. DJ had already finished his plate.

At nine, DJ's night replacement rang the doorbell. Only this time it wasn't the silent Officer Colton, it was Detective Masterson at the door.

I looked up from the rerun of *Gilmore Girls* I was watching.

"You're staying tonight?" I asked, surprised when he walked in. Mom and Dad were back in their bedroom talking, and I'd heard the word *UCLA* used, so I figured it was about Mike.

DJ closed and locked the door behind Detective Masterson, and they both sat on the sofa beside me.

"What's this?" the detective asked.

"*Gilmore Girls*," DJ answered before I could.

Detective Masterson looked at DJ and then snorted.

"Excuse me," I said. "This show is a wonderful satire on life and women and small towns, and I happen to love it."

"Sure, sure," Detective Masterson said. "Whatever you say, Kate."

"I can pick a girlier show," I threatened, waving the remote. "I think that *Barefoot Contessa* is on right now."

DJ almost jumped at me. "No!"

"No more mocking my show?"

DJ shook his head violently. "No more mocking your show. Kent?" He elbowed Detective Masterson.

There was the Kent thing again. My brain could not process that Detective Masterson's name was Kent to his friends.

Kent.

He grinned. "Consider the mocking over and done with." He leaned back against the sofa cushions. "So, what does the famous Kate Carter have going on this weekend? I mean, aside from the parade with the governor and dinner with the mayor?"

"A parade?" I moaned, muting the TV right in the middle of one of Lorelai Gilmore's famous word battles with Rory.

"Just a short one." Detective Masterson grinned at me. "Just around Main Street and up to Cherry Road."

I growled under my breath. "And what am I supposed to do on this parade?"

"Oh, you know, the usual. Smile, wave, blow kisses to the eligible young bachelors in town, and toss candy to the babies."

Detective Masterson was grinning ear to ear and enjoying this entirely too much.

"Do I have to?" I asked.

"You have to." Detective Masterson picked up the remote and changed the channel to KCL, where the too-white-toothed Ted Deffle was doing the evening news.

"A six-pack of Diet Coke was found to be missing from McSweeny's earlier today," he was saying.

I looked at DJ and the detective. "Do you guys ever worry about your job security in this town?"

DJ nodded. "Every day."

"I used to," Detective Masterson said. "But then I realized that without me, the three guys who drink the weekend away at Barney's would be out there driving drunk, Mrs. Lainger would have no one to call whenever she thought her house was getting broken into, and little Lacey Cutler's kitten would have been eaten by the next-door neighbor's dog on a daily basis for the last three years."

DJ looked over Detective Masterson to me again. "Like I said, every day."

Chapter Eight

SATURDAY MORNING DAWNED BRIGHT AND BEAUTIFUL, and I woke up to the smell of pancakes.

Pancakes?

I sniffed confusedly and stumbled out of bed, grabbing my change of clothes and heading for the bathroom. Five minutes later, I had on presentable sweats and my teeth were brushed.

So long, Saturday mornings in my pajamas.

I made it to the kitchen, yawning. Mom and Dad were nowhere to be found, but DJ was blissfully eating a huge stack of pancakes, and Detective Masterson was busy flipping more.

"Morning, Kate," he hummed. "Pancake?"

Miss Yeager, should she be the one, was turning out to be a lucky girl. I nodded and sat down at the table next to DJ.

"Sleep good?" DJ asked me.

"Yes," I lied. Truthfully, I dreamt that John X's mug shot had been chasing me in the governor's parade car. He kept catching all the candy I threw and knocking over my parents and Maddy, trying to catch up to me.

"You didn't sound like you slept well," the detective said, coming over with a plate stacked three pancakes high and setting it in front of me. "You were mewling all night."

Well, this was embarrassing. I wanted my door closed at night like before this whole fiasco, so the only person who knew whether I made noise when I slept was Lolly, who usually slept on the floor by my bed.

I glared at the detective and then dug into the pancakes.

They were delicious and try as I might, I couldn't stay mad at someone who created such fluffy, tasty delights.

"Good?" he asked, sitting in one of the empty chairs, sipping from a cup of coffee.

"Kent, if I'd known you were such a good wife, I would have married you years ago." DJ grinned, shoving another forkful of pancakes in his mouth.

Detective Masterson took another sip of coffee and pulled the morning paper over. "Sadly, you're not my type. But thank you for the proposal."

"Who is your type?" I asked, squirting more syrup on my stack. "Miss Yeager?"

DJ perked up at that one. "The woman at the school?" He looked at me. "Your art teacher?"

I nodded.

"Oh, look at the headline," the detective said, not answering DJ's question.

DJ winked at me.

"'Local Hero to Be Featured in Tomorrow's May Day Parade'," Detective Masterson read.

I yanked the paper from him. There was my horrific yearbook picture slathered all over the front page.

It was like other pictures of me just didn't exist. I groaned.

"Now, now. Let me see your smile for the adoring public, Kate." Detective Masterson grinned over his coffee.

"Look at this picture," I said, pointing to the front page. "Do I really look like that in person?"

DJ studied it for a minute. "You are kind of squinting all weird there."

Mom walked in the kitchen, hair styled, makeup on, and

wearing jeans and a Western button-down shirt. "Good morning, Katie-Kin," she said, ruffling her hand through my hair.

I suddenly realized why Lolly always leaned into us whenever we petted her.

"Morning, guys," Mom said, nodding to the policemen.

"Morning," they chimed simultaneously.

Detective Masterson stood. "Pancakes, ma'am?" he asked, pouring batter onto the griddle.

Mom nodded and sat beside me. "Thanks, Detective."

I almost laughed. Here it was Saturday morning. My mother was completely dressed before ten, I had a detective in the police force serving pancakes and coffee to my family, and a police officer sleeping outside my bedroom on an air mattress.

Life could not get weirder.

Dad walked in then, 9mm strapped to his waist.

Then again, perhaps I spoke too soon.

Dad started squinting through the barely cracked kitchen blinds, and DJ elbowed me.

"That's the expression you've got right here," he whispered, pointing to the newspaper.

I sighed.

"Anything happen last night?" Dad asked the detective.

Detective Masterson shook his head, flipping the pancakes. "No, sir. It was very quiet." He looked toward the front door. "Although we did get something this morning."

Dad immediately walked out of the kitchen and came back holding the hugest bouquet of flowers I'd ever seen in my life.

"Wow," Mom and I chimed together.

"Who's it from?" I asked, clambering off my chair and over to where Dad was struggling to set it down on the counter. I ended up needing to get my chair and stand on it to see the top of the arrangement.

"See a card?" Dad asked.

"No. Oh wait," I said, pulling the tiniest white envelope from the huge monstrosity of tulips, daisies, roses, violets, and lilies.

It simply said *Kate* on the front.

I was just about to open it when Detective Masterson took it from me. "Sorry, Kate. I have to inspect everything that comes through that front door."

He opened it, read it, snorted, and then passed it to me.

I stood on the chair and started reading.

Dearest Kate —

"What's it say?" Mom asked. "Read it out loud."

I was suddenly very happy that we didn't live in the time of that *Pride and Prejudice* book. I was only imagining what it would be like to get a romantic letter from Mr. Darcy and then have to read it out loud to my mother.

I hopped off the chair. In this case, Detective Masterson had already read it. It couldn't get much worse than that.

" 'Dearest Kate,' " I started again.

Dad frowned at me and Mom started getting all sappy.

DJ was snickering behind his coffee cup, I was pretty sure.

" 'In gratitude for your civic service, thankfulness for your generous spirit, and hopefulness for our eventual meeting, I trust you are as overwhelmed by this bouquet as I am by your bravery. Thank you.' "

It was signed *Sincerely, Ted Deffle, KCL News.*

I felt my nose wrinkling up.

"Ted Deffle?" Dad choked on his coffee. "He's like twenty years older than you! Is that even legal?" He looked at DJ.

"To send a girl a bouquet of roses out of thankfulness?" DJ asked. He looked at Detective Masterson and shrugged. "I guess so."

"I would imagine the honorable Ted just wants to secure an interview spot with Kate," Detective Masterson said, handing Mom and Dad their pancakes. "Coffee?"

I sat back down at the table. Ted Deffle sent me flowers.

Ugh.

Maddy was not going to believe this.

"Another pancake, Kate?" Detective Masterson asked.

"Please." And keep them coming.

By the time we were heading to the mayor's house that night, I'd received another three bouquets. One from the local paper, one from the South Woodhaven Falls Rotary Club, and another one from the KCL staff.

I'd also gotten seventeen thank-you notes in the mailbox from people all over the St. Louis area. One lady claimed that she'd seen a man who matched my drawing in her grocery store last week buying processed cheese crackers.

"I wondered at the time, but it makes sense now," she'd written.

I figured that meant criminals must eat processed cheese crackers, and I asked DJ if I should add that to my Jailbird's menu.

He said that in his experience, most of them seemed to prefer the peanut butter crackers over the cheese, but he'd also known of at least three high-profile crooks who were lactose intolerant, so maybe that threw off the count.

I added both cheese and peanut butter crackers to the menu.

DJ was driving us over in an unmarked black Tahoe, but it was definitely a police vehicle on the inside. Mom and I sat in the back, and Dad sat up front with DJ.

I was wearing a light blue and brown dress that was entirely too summery for the spring weather. My shins were getting cold. I'd put a brown sweater over my arms, but now I was wishing there was a way to put sweater sleeves over my legs without looking like a complete fashion accident.

I think those are called leg warmers, but in my experience, those were better left to the girls who thought Britney Spears was a style icon and it was best for me to leave those alone. Particularly with a summer dress.

I'd never been to the mayor's house before, but as we pulled through the gate leading to the huge front lawn, I was suddenly overwhelmed by the money to be made in politics.

"I had no idea he lived in such a huge house," I said. "Tax dollars?"

"Family money," Dad answered me.

Maybe it's a life of schmoozing that pays off in the end. Mayor Arnold Walinski was a world-class butter-upper.

If that was a word.

DJ parked the car in front of the mansion and we all piled out, greeted by two guys whom I assumed were security and two dogs that I assumed were part pit bull.

"Miss Carter?" one of them said to me, putting out his hand. "Pleased to meet you. The mayor and his family have been looking forward to meeting you."

We followed the man into the house and into a huge dining room. Mayor Walinski was standing there next to a bleached-blonde woman and two dark-haired kids who were probably in elementary school.

"Greetings!" Arnold Walinski said. "Welcome to my home!"

It was all very awkward. The bleached lady looked bored to tears, the kids were too busy poking each other for me to remember their names or them to remember mine, and dinner salads were busy wilting on the gold-circled china plates.

"Please, sit," Arnold said, motioning to the table.

DJ stayed in the room, but he didn't sit down, since there wasn't a place setting for him. I started wondering if he felt like hired help.

"So, Kate, once again, I just want to say thank you for everything that you've done to keep our fair town in its safe environment," Arnold said, while his wife picked at her salad and the kids threw olives at each other.

I'm not sure when people will finally realize that this was all a big accident and all I did was draw what I was told to draw.

"You are welcome," I said, because it was starting to get old protesting.

And then we sat there in silence. Dad was done with his salad and Mom was finishing the last couple of bites. I was pretending to eat, but pushing it around instead. It was made with that bitter lettuce stuff and I was an iceberg kind of a girl.

Tasteless and crunchy. That was how I liked my lettuce.

A lady brought out the next course, which Arnold declared to be lamb.

And it looked like I was going hungry tonight, alongside DJ. There was no way I was going to eat a cute fluffy lamb, I don't care how tender it was.

"Isn't this amazing?" Arnold said, breaking the silence, chomping away. "Our cook is Grecian and she makes the most excellent lamb dishes."

"Wonderful," Mom said, lightly picking at it.

"So, tell me more about yourself, Kate," Arnold said.

I looked up at him and shrugged. "I'm a junior."

"I knew that. What do you like to do? Well, besides drawing, I mean," he said, laughing.

What did I like to do? Between homework, Maddy, and E!, I didn't have a lot of free time.

I shrugged again. "Hang out, I guess." I was realizing that aside from art and championing for non-soggy Crispix, I had zero hobbies.

No one was ever going to describe me as a well-rounded student.

"Well, that's very interesting!" Arnold burst. "Have you ever thought about a career in politics? Pretty much, you just hang out with people and try to garner their vote." Then he laughed a creepy staccato laugh.

My dad just paused right in the middle of eating his lamb steak. "What about protecting our people from total government control? What about campaigning on upholding the Constitution? What about freedom of the peoples?"

Politics were never a good dinner conversation when my dad was involved.

Arnold immediately went into apology/super schmooze mode. "Well, yes, yes, *of course* we have to work to protect the freedoms of the people. I was merely suggesting that Kate might be good at it considering her people skills and obvious good head on her shoulders, *never* that a politician's only job duty was to hang out with people."

"Uh-huh," Dad said.

We finished the meal in near silence.

"Thank you for coming tonight," Arnold said after all the plates had been cleared. "My family really enjoyed getting to meet all of you."

I wasn't sure his family agreed with that assessment, but we nodded. "Thank you for having us," I said.

Then we climbed back into the unmarked black Tahoe and headed back home.

"Kate, if you ever think of going into politics ..." Dad threatened.

"He served lamb," I said at the same time, getting sad for the poor fluffy baby.

"Those poor children are being raised in an atmosphere that is entirely inappropriate for proper growth," Mom said.

DJ listened to all of us and then grinned. "Successful evening, I take it."

"Could you please stop by Walton's? I need a burger," I said. I may not be able to eat lamb, but I can definitely eat beef. I think it has to do with calling the meat by a different name than what I call the animal.

DJ changed the direction he was driving.

"Politicians," Dad muttered under his breath, using the same tone of voice he used when he talked about the Braille print on

ATM machines. Anytime Dad wanted to point out the direction he felt humanity was headed in, he always talked about Braille on drive-thru ATM machines. "If that's not a straight shot toward stupidity, I don't know what is," he would say.

"Well, Kate, tomorrow is the May Day parade and I got word from Deputy Slalom that you can start talking to the press now. We've scheduled a press conference for tomorrow after the parade. How does that sound?" DJ asked.

It sounded like a day better off spent in the Pit of Despair, like on *The Princess Bride*, but I didn't say that. "Fine," I groaned.

DJ pulled into Walton's drive-through and I told him I wanted a cheeseburger and fries and then passed him a five dollar bill.

"I'd like a cheeseburger, fries, and double-decker chicken sandwich," he ordered.

A few minutes later, we pulled into our driveway and I settled on our sofa, unwrapping my greasy burger and turning the TV to KCL, fully anticipating a shot of our front door to be part of the news again tonight.

They had a different picture headlining, though.

"Good evening, ladies and gentlemen, and thank you for watching KCL News, the news you can trust!" Ted Deffle said, grinning that nearly blinding white smile. I ran my tongue over my teeth. I might need to go get some of those whitening strips before the press conference tomorrow.

"Tonight, we take you to the lair of a killer," he said, all dramatically. I took a bite of my cheeseburger and watched as the picture of a different front door appeared next to Ted's head.

"This is the reputed house of the killer known as John X."

I sat up a little straighter and turned the volume up a little louder. DJ came in and sat on the couch with me, eating his chicken sandwich.

"Police in the Greater St. Louis Area have been painstakingly combing through every belonging in this suburban home, looking for evidence in the four deaths of women in the surrounding area."

A map showed the four counties around St. Louis where John X had claimed lives.

"We're going live to Candace Olstrom at the scene. Candace?"

"Hi, Ted," squeaky blonde Candace said, standing outside a house marked off with bright yellow caution tape. The whole street was dark except for the news crew lights on Candace. "I'm here outside the house that police now know was the headquarters for the serial killer known as John X. Earlier today I got to talk to several of the neighbors to see what they knew."

It switched from a live feed to a tape of earlier when it was still light outside.

"Yeah, I knew 'im," one man said around a huge wad of pink bubblegum. "'E was always out in 'is yard, workin' on some old mower or sometin. 'E weren't too friendly. One of my kids 'it a baseball back there and 'e wouldn't give it back." Then the man spit the huge wad of bubblegum into his yard.

I loved how news crews out here always managed to find the pride and joy of the population to interview.

"I met him once," a lady carrying a baby said next. The baby kept trying to grab Candace's microphone. "Stop it, Lucy. I got a package that was his, so I took it over. He seemed friendly, if not a little distant. Lucy, cut it out. Who knew he was a killer? I never lock my doors, I never worry about my safety. Lucy, I swear ... I'll tell you what, though, I'm locking my doors tonight, that's for sure and certain."

"Top of the crop tonight," DJ muttered.

I smiled.

Then they switched to a picture of John X in prison, and my smile faded. He was sitting on a cot staring out of bars, and he didn't look happy at all.

Mad might be a better word.

Or livid.

He hadn't used a razor and he looked kind of dirty. He didn't really resemble the man I drew in art class as much.

"Authorities say they've uncovered several incriminating pieces that will be used in the trial against John X. Ted?"

"Thanks, Candace. In other news, the local heroine who helped aid in the capture of John X will be appearing in the May Day parade tomorrow alongside the governor, and we also will finally get a chance to talk to the notorious Kate Carter afterwards."

They were showing that awful yearbook picture of me again, but to be honest, I wasn't really paying attention.

All I could see was John X sitting behind those bars. Livid.

At me.

"Kate?" DJ asked.

I blinked and looked up at him. Suddenly, the cold, half-eaten, greasy burger in my hands didn't look so appetizing anymore. I wadded it up in the paper.

"You okay?" he asked.

I nodded. "Fine." It was better not to worry the policeman just doing his job. If I was going to tell anyone my worries, it was going to be Lolly. Mom would try to do her psychoanalyzing thing on me, Dad would start in about Miss Yeager, and Maddy would just go all drama queen.

Lolly was a dumb dog sometimes, but she was a good listener.

DJ twisted his lips like he didn't believe me, but he nodded. "Your call," he said. "Ready for the parade tomorrow? Let me see your wave."

I just rolled my eyes. "So ready. And no, you can't see my wave."

Ted was now showing clips of the families of the women John X had killed.

"We are so thankful that this man has been brought to justice for the murder of my wife," one man said, a teary teenage son and daughter beside him. He had to gather himself for a minute and then continued. "We will never heal completely, but with God all things are possible. Thank you, Kate Carter and the fine men and women of the St. Louis area police team. May God bless you and yours." Then he had to step away, wiping his eyes and holding onto his kids.

They looked like they were a nice family. Why did bad things always seem to happen to nice people?

DJ was watching me again.

"What?" I asked, looking over at him.

He squinted at me. "You did a good thing, Kate. I just want you to remember that. And I know you're freaking out right now, but remember that he's in prison and you are safe. Okay?"

I liked that DJ was young enough to use *freaking out* in its proper context. My dad tried to do that once and it didn't turn out quite so well.

I didn't like that DJ could read me like an open book. In a lot of ways, he was like the brother I always wanted and never got in Mike. Mike was always too concerned over things that concerned him.

Never things that concerned his annoying little sister.

I nodded to DJ. "I'm fine," I said again.

"Sure," he said. "I know."

I watched a couple more of the victim's families' interviews and tried to stop grinding my teeth. "Just fine," I mumbled again.

Chapter Nine

SUNDAY MORNING AND MOM, DAD, DJ, AND I WERE ALL sitting in one of the very uncomfortable pews at South Woodhaven Falls First Baptist Church.

Which I thought was an entirely-too-long-name for a building that could probably only hold about two hundred people.

Maybe.

We were handed a piece of paper with the order of the service on it when we sat down, and right as we sat an old lady slammed a chord down so hard on the organ at the front of the sanctuary that all four of us jumped.

About a third of the people in the room stood up then and gathered on the stage, wearing what looked like something flamboyant monks would wear or maybe something that a color-blind school would use for graduation. And they were all holding books in front of them and clearing their throats.

"Join us, won't you, in standing and singing Hymn 239," a man also wearing the monk outfit said into a microphone. The lady at the organ started busting out a long chord succession and then the people in front starting singing.

"Lord, who dost give to thy church," they all started, and that's where they lost me.

Who was dost? Or maybe it was a what?

Dad was standing stoically and looking at the choir in a mix of peevishness and boredom. Mom was fumbling with a book she pulled out of the back of the pew in front of her, which I realized was a book of music. And DJ was squinting at another one of the books, trying to follow along.

The organ lady finished with an ear-shattering ending and then started up again. "Hymn 197!" the same man yelled out. "And sing with joy!"

"We're marching to Zion," the people around me and on the stage sang loudly. "Beautiful, beautiful, Zion!"

I'd never heard of Zion, and other than it sounding very similar to a large cat found in our local zoo, I wasn't sure what it was.

Again, another eardrum-splitting finale, and then we all sat and listened to a man in a poor-fitting suit who said "amen" after every sentence.

Including one that made a reference to McSweeny's market. I'd never heard McSweeny's market amened before.

"And I said to a woman in the middle of McSweeny's market, 'Woman! You can have peace!' Amen?"

"Amen!" the people around us shouted, making me jump yet again.

I tried to subtly look around while the man was talking. There were primarily people in what I would guess were their late sixties, maybe early seventies around us. I didn't see anyone who was my age, and I only saw one other couple who was my parents' ages.

After the final "amen" had been shouted, the organ lady took up her post again and everyone started milling around the room, talking very loudly so they could be heard over the organ.

"Well, hello there!" a tiny old woman with hair that was whiter than anything OxiClean had ever treated said to us when we got ready to leave. She stuck her hand out to my dad. "I'm Sister Elizabeth Parker. And you are?"

It would be very hard to go through your whole life with the nickname "sister." She seemed to take it well, though.

"Dale," my dad said gruffly.

Sister Elizabeth Parker grinned brightly. "Welcome to South Woodhaven Falls First Baptist Church!" she said with more oomph than the organ lady played with.

And that was a lot of oomph.

Especially for a little woman like Sister Elizabeth.

"I'm Claire," Mom said, shaking the woman's hand. "This is my daughter, Kate, and ... our friend, DJ."

It was a nice save and DJ smiled.

"Well, it's very nice to meet you all. I must say, I haven't seen a hair untouched by the Master Grayer in this service since 1998!" She stuck her hands on her tiny hips for emphasis. "Most of you young folk tend to go for the late service. Contemporary music and that stuff that hurts my ears." Then she grinned all big at us.

Despite the fact that I'm pretty sure she was one of the loudest "amen"-ers behind us, I decided I kind of liked Sister Elizabeth. She seemed spunky.

"Well, now. You fine folks should sure come back now, you hear?"

"Yes, ma'am, we certainly will," Mom said.

Judging by Dad's expression, I didn't think that was what he was planning for next Sunday.

We walked out to the foyer before the exit, and I finally saw a group of people my age moving toward the sanctuary.

And my mouth dropped.

At the center of the group, loudly telling a joke that had the other nine kids laughing hysterically — none other than Justin Walters from art.

Aka Silent Justin.

I just stood there gaping at him. I don't know if he felt the complete shock in my gaze melting toward him or what, but suddenly he stopped talking and looked over at me.

And blinked. "Kate?" he said.

Apparently I gasped from the total surprise at the first time I'd heard him say my name, which made DJ and my father panic.

"What? What?" Dad shouted, grabbing my right arm.

"Let's get you to the car immediately," DJ said, grabbing my left arm.

I wrestled out of their reaches and Justin walked over.

Smiling.

"Hi, Kate," he said easily, like we were good friends and talked all the time. "How are you? I didn't know you came to first service."

At this point, I was waiting for either Ashton Kutcher to arrive on the scene and announce that I had just been *Punk'd* or for Justin to introduce himself as Justin's previously-unheard-of identical twin, Dustin.

I glanced around, but I did not see Ashton or another Justin lookalike, and the Justin who was in front of me was now giving me a very weird look.

"You okay?" he asked.

"You speak?" I asked.

He said, "What?"

"I have never heard you talk, ever," I said.

Dad and DJ exchanged a look and then walked with Mom a few feet away. I appreciated the privacy. Should Ashton Kutcher appear, it would be nice to not embarrass my entire family.

Justin shrugged. "Sometimes I like being quiet."

He said it the same way he would say he sometimes liked Canadian bacon on his pizza. Nonchalant.

"Sometimes? We're almost halfway through the school year," I said.

He shrugged again. "So a lot of times. Especially at school."

"How come?"

Yet another shrug. I was beginning to feel the ache in my shoulders. "I don't know," he said. "Guess I don't have much to say." Then he changed the subject. "So, when did you start coming to SWF First Baptist?"

"This morning," I said.

"Oh. Well, you should come to the late service next time. It's more contemporary."

"Meaning no organ?" I asked quietly.

He shook his head. "No organ. Guitars, drums, keyboard."

"And the Amen-ers?"

He crinkled up his forehead. "What?"

"Never mind."

He just nodded at me. The group he'd been talking to came over and he smiled at them. "Okay, well, I have to go. But I'll see you tomorrow at school. Bye, Kate."

Then he and his group disappeared into the sanctuary.

Talking.

I shook my head slightly. Don't visions typically happen around churches or church people? Maybe I just had a vision.

A vision of what could be.

"Who was that?" Mom asked as I walked over to where they stood next to the door.

"A guy from art class."

Dad mumbled something about artsy boys under his breath but I chose to ignore it.

DJ looked at his watch. "It's almost ten thirty and you are supposed to be at the parade grounds in an hour," he told me.

"Oh, yay," I said, sighing.

"Try to contain your enthusiasm, Kate. We are in a public building. You don't want to cause a scene." Mom grinned, leading the way outside.

A parade. I hated even going to a parade. Being in one had to be a zillion times worse.

I had just walked out the door, squinting into the sun, when someone said, "Kate Carter?"

I turned and it was a lady in her forties I didn't recognize. "Yes?"

She gasped and clasped her hands to her chest. "Kate Carter?" she screeched again. "*The* Kate Carter?"

"And it's time to go," DJ said, quickly grabbing for my elbow.

"Oh my gosh, I am *so* thankful for you!" the woman yelled. "You are a hero, young lady, do you hear me?"

I was pretty certain that everyone in the neighborhood could hear her. I managed a short smile before I got hustled into the black Tahoe by DJ and Dad.

"You are too recognizable," DJ huffed as he climbed into the driver's seat.

"I squinted," I said, sighing.

"What?" Mom said.

"I squinted. Like in my picture in the yearbook." I squeezed my eyes halfway shut to show her.

Mom waved her hand. "Please. Your yearbook picture does not look like that."

"Does too. Check when we get home. Why else would she have recognized me only after I was staring into the sun?"

DJ cleared his throat. "She is kind of squinty in the picture."

"See? Thank you, DJ."

Dad looked out the passenger window. "Yet another reason I carry at churches."

We all looked at him. "Carry what?" I asked cautiously.

Dad turned toward me in the backseat. "My pistol. I've been carrying constantly since all this started. You can never be too careful, Kate. Did you hear those people at church? Yelling 'amen' at the preacher?"

"I think they were encouraging him," Mom said.

"Constantly being told to be quiet is not encouraging someone, Claire."

DJ opened his mouth to respond and then apparently thought better of it. "The parade," he said, changing the subject. "Kate, we're going to have continuous security on you at the parade, so there is nothing to worry about there."

I think he was speaking more toward my dad and his 9mm than he was to me.

"Okay," I said, and looked out the window. We were driving past Main right then and the town was already being littered with tons of May Day décor. Huge papier-mâché daisies, Chinese lanterns made to look like giant rosebuds, and yards and yards of pastel-colored streamers were hung everywhere along the street.

Soon, all the people in South Woodhaven Falls who owned an antique car would line up for the parade, and the school's marching band and cheerleading squad was going to perform. Mr. McSweeny closed his market and put on a clown costume most years. People even came and sold cotton candy and hot dogs.

It was a real event if you liked events.

I, however, did not like events. I spent most May Day parades catching up on homework or practicing my sketching. It was going to be a long day.

The governor owned a 1937 Packard convertible. Which if you were into cars was apparently a big deal because I guess that car was worth a lot of money. DJ told me on the way home that the governor was going to drive, his wife was going to be in the passenger seat, and me, DJ, and two other policemen were going to be in the backseat.

So it was going to be a crowded and claustrophobic long day. Great.

DJ stopped at my house, and yet again there were news vans in front. I bit back the groan. Weren't they going to get enough of the squinty-eyed heroine at the parade? Could they not wait until then?

"Hustle in," DJ said, pushing me in front of him and into my house while all the reporters yelled my name.

We got inside and Lolly came over, wagging her tail and looking at me all friendly-like.

I knelt down and gave her a hug. "Thank you for not speaking," I told her.

She licked my hand.

I had already decided that I was going to wear my favorite pair of dark-rinsed jeans and a forest green short-sleeved shirt. It was a gorgeous day outside and I really didn't think I'd need a jacket sitting in the back of a convertible.

I carried my clothes to the bathroom and changed quickly, trying not to mess up my hair from church. I'd run a straightener through it early this morning. Hopefully, it would stay straight and not get all frizzy like it was prone to do.

I touched up my makeup and stepped back to look in the mirror.

Well. It would have to do.

Mom was coming down the hall when I opened the bathroom door. "All set?" she asked, pulling a tube of lipstick from her purse.

I nodded as she smeared the bright raspberry color all over her lips. "You want some?" she asked when she finished.

"No, thanks." I wasn't a lipstick person. Lip gloss occasionally. When Maddy made me wear it. But never lipstick.

"Are you sure? Just add a little bit of color?" Mom asked, pointing the tube at my face.

I shook my head. "I don't think so."

"Girls, you need to get something to eat!" Dad yelled from the kitchen. "We have to leave in half an hour!"

My dad was nothing if not on time. My mother was one of those people who believed in fashionable lateness. Dad always said that if she were meant to be fashionable, she wouldn't have married an engineer.

Wise words, I always thought.

Dad was standing in the kitchen spreading mayo on two slices of bread. He was wearing jeans and a polo shirt. "Want a deli sandwich?" he asked when I walked in.

"Um." Now to decide how to answer this one. Yes, I did want a sandwich, but I didn't want Dad to make it for me. Dad uses way too much mayo for my tastes.

"Yeah, but I'll make it," I finally said. "Go ahead and finish yours."

Dad shrugged and stacked a healthy helping of deli-sliced turkey, tomatoes, lettuce, and pickles on his bread. By the time he finished, it was a good four inches high.

"Now that," Dad said, proudly. "That is a sandwich."

"Nicely done."

"Sure you don't want me to make yours?" he asked.

"Very sure." Especially if the outcome was going to be bigger than my head.

I slathered some mustard and mayo on two slices of bread, added a little bit of meat, one tomato, and two lettuce leaves. When I got to the table, Dad just shook his head.

"Weakling," he said.

"The camera adds ten pounds, Dad," I said, sitting across from him.

"Good. Then you'll finally look somewhat healthy."

I took a bite of my sandwich. All of the women on my mother's side of the family were tiny. I think Mom was the tallest and she was only five foot three. My grandma was four foot nine. And she maybe weighed ninety-five pounds.

Dad, though, had a coworker who discovered three years ago that his daughter was anorexic, and now Dad was completely panicked that I might be too. I kept telling him about my love of cookies and carbs in general, but I don't think he believed me.

If I had to change anything about my appearance, I'd change my height. To taller. Much taller. It got old having to tilt my head all the time.

Mom and DJ came into the kitchen then. Mom made a quick lunch of crackers, lunch meat, and cheese, and DJ made a sandwich.

"We're going to wait here for Kent to come. He's going to drive with us," DJ said, swallowing a bite of his huge sandwich.

I wondered if Miss Yeager was going to be at the parade. She was all nostalgic about the weird traditions this town had.

"Where should Claire and I be?" Dad asked.

DJ said, "You can stand wherever you like. We've got another guy coming to shadow you two, but I think everything will be fine today. The parade ends at two and the press conference starts at

City Hall thirty minutes later, so if I were you, I'd try to find a spot close to there if you can."

Mom nodded. "Wow, Katie-Kin. City Hall. That's pretty impressive!"

I sighed. "What exactly do they want me to say at this press conference?" I wasn't good in front of cameras anyway — as evidenced by my yearbook picture — so I had no idea how I was going to be in front of several and still have coherent things to say.

"Just tell them about the drawing," DJ said. "Don't mention anyone's name and don't say anything about where you live." He shrugged. "It'll be fine, Kate."

"Easy for you to say. You don't have to be in front of the cameras."

"No, but Detective Masterson will be up there with you, so at least you won't be alone in front of the cameras." Then he got very serious. "And Kate? The most important thing you need to remember?"

I waited. "Yeah?"

"Don't squint."

I threw my one tomato slice at his face.

Chapter Ten

THE GOVERNOR WAS ALREADY THERE WHEN WE GOT TO the beginning of Main. Our governor was a nice, round man. And I couldn't think of another way to describe him. He was just very ... round.

His face was round, his torso was round. He even did his hair in that comb-over style, so that even looked round once a nice breeze kicked up.

But he was nice and as far as I knew a good politician, and he couldn't remember my name to save his life.

"Sarah!" he said warmly when we walked over to his old-fashioned convertible.

I looked around, but my mom's name is Claire and the two of us were the only girls there beside the governor's wife, whose name is Patricia.

Detective Masterson, who had picked us all up a few minutes ago, leaned closer to the governor. "Kate," he said quietly.

The governor shook his head. "My apologies." Then he started over. "Kate!" Once more, the warmth just flowed. "My thankfulness and appreciation to you, my dear!"

I nodded, smiling. I liked our governor. His wife was a tiny little thing with grayish-blonde highlights cut into a Jackie O style. She smiled at me in one of those "yeah, what he said" smiles.

Our town does not have a very big Main Street, so in order for the parade to last two hours, we had to drive five miles an hour the whole way.

People were milling around everywhere. Finishing the decorations, parking their antique cars in a parking lot across the street so they could get in line a little later, already snacking on foot-long corn dogs and Dippin' Dots ice cream.

Which looked really good, and I decided that after our spot in the parade was over I was definitely getting one of the corn dogs.

There were a few speakers placed strategically down Main Street and all of a sudden they kicked on. Dean Martin started crooning *Ain't That a Kick in the Head*, and my mom started whistling to it.

"I love Dino!" Mom said.

The governor nodded appreciatively. "I certainly agree. He was one of the best musical artists of the entire last century."

"Americana would have been much different without him." Mom sighed.

"How is security going to work here?" Dad asked, apparently not caring about Dino and his effect on Americana.

Detective Masterson took over. "Governor, you and your wife will be driving. I'm going to have Kate sit on the top of the trunk—"

I blinked. "What?" I said.

Detective Masterson kept talking. "—with Officer Kirkpatrick and Officer DeWeise on either side of her."

So I was between DJ and another officer, a Mr. DeWeise, who looked like he was probably a lineman back in his college football days. He smiled nicely at me and I noticed the missing right eye tooth.

Wrong sport. Maybe hockey?

"Meanwhile, I've got another four guys coming. Two will be driving in a squad car in front of you and me and two other guys will be directly behind you in another squad car." The detective looked at Dad. "How does that sound?"

It looked like it pained Dad to admit that it did sound good. "And where should Claire and I be?"

"You can just feel free to enjoy the parade. Get a Dippin' Dots or a cotton candy or something."

Considering that Dad is about as excited about parades as I am, he handled the day's activities well. "Fine," he said quietly. "We'll wait here until Kate is leaving."

"Perfectly okay," Detective Masterson said.

At ten minutes before the parade was scheduled to start, all of us had to take our place in the car. I perched myself precariously on the trunk of the car with my feet dangling into the backseat. The metal of the car and the leather on the seats were hot and I was glad I'd opted to not wear a skirt, since the back of my bare legs would have been touching it.

DJ and Officer DeWeise were going to be roasting by the end of the parade, since they were in full uniform complete with their bulletproof vests.

"Are those heavy?" I asked as DJ adjusted his.

He thought about it and then shook his head. "They're pretty lightweight. They make custom ones now, but South Woodhaven Falls doesn't have a big enough budget to cover getting those for all of us. Especially since you've heard about our daily adrenaline rush of getting cats out of pit bull's teeth."

I grinned.

"But these ones aren't too heavy. Just bulky more than anything."

Officer DeWeise squinted at me. "We might have one that will fit you at the station. We've got a girl officer who left for maternity leave and she was about your size."

"Before or after the maternity part?" I asked, wondering if I should take a more proactive approach to my workout routine.

DJ rolled his eyes. "Before, Kate. Please don't tell me you are like other girls and all uptight and overly concerned about your appearance."

"I'm sorry, have you seen my yearbook picture?" I said.

He grinned.

"What yearbook picture?" Officer DeWeise asked.

"The one that's headlining everything they ever say about me," I groaned. "I look like this." I squinched up my eyes at him.

He tilted his head. "Actually, yeah, that does look kind of familiar."

I sighed. "Anyway, I think I have some small right to be a little bit concerned about my appearance now."

DJ conceded with a shrug. "Whatever. Did you at least bring sunglasses?"

I brought them in my purse, which I'd stuck below my feet on the passenger seat. "Got them. Think I should put them on right now?" The road ahead was pretty shaded for the first mile.

Officer DeWeise shook his head. "Just wait. Practice smiling with your eyes open for the first little bit."

DJ thought that was hilarious.

Our police force employed a regular lineup of comedians. I shook my head. The governor and his wife were climbing into the front seat and Mom waved at me.

"Smile pretty!" she said all happily. She loved the parade, so I was imagining she was just excited to get Dad out there without major arguments about how it wasn't even a real holiday.

"You listen to the cops," Dad told me. "And pay attention. Keep your eyes open."

"Yes, sir," I said.

"Don't worry, sir, I just told her the same thing," Officer DeWeise said.

The governor started up the car and we lurched once, nearly throwing all three of us into the backseat.

"Whoa!" The governor said. "Sorry about that, folks. Forgot the clutch was on. Here we go!"

We started chugging along Main Street, and I have to admit, I was amazed at how many people showed up to this kind of stuff.

People were milling around and everywhere I looked, I kept seeing foot-long corn dogs.

My stomach growled.

"You cannot be hungry," DJ said. "We just ate."

"Those corn dogs look really good," I said.

"Don't forget to wave, Kate!" Patricia, the governor's wife, told me.

I nodded and lifted my hand as we came to a section where people were actually lined up to see the parade, not just to flaunt their foot-long corn dogs.

The squad car in front of us was keeping a nice casual pace of five miles an hour, so I got to get a real good look at those corn dogs. A few people saw me and started waving.

"Kate Carter!" one lady yelled. "It's Kate Carter!"

"Thank you, Kate!" a man hollered from the other side of the street.

Soon there were probably a couple hundred or more people gathered along the sidewalk, and a chant started.

"Kate is great! Kate is great! Kate is great!"

I just waved and focused on smiling with my eyes open. Though, I have to admit, I liked that chant better than the one that Sean and Kyle Prestwick yelled at me in the second grade. They were twins, and they were both evil. They would always say, "Kate, Kate, Gator Bait!" every time I passed by them.

This was especially traumatizing because I believed then that there were really alligators in the Mississippi River, which is fairly close to South Woodhaven Falls. We took a field trip there every year from kindergarten to the fifth grade. And every year we looked at the same portion of the flood wall and heard how high the river had gotten in years past. And every year, the Prestwick boys would pretend that they were going to throw me in while I screamed and pleaded for my life.

I was not sad at all when they up and moved to Kansas City.

I blinked back to the present right as someone threw something large at the car and I ducked, squealing.

DJ caught it and laughed. It was a bouquet of roses.

"Thank you!" I yelled.

"Kate is great! Kate is great!"

I kept waving.

"I feel ignored," Officer DeWeise said a few minutes later, when everyone was still chanting "Kate is great!" and applauding.

"So do I," the governor said, smiling at me in the rearview mirror. "But goodness knows, you deserve it, Kate. Ever thought about running for office?"

I shook my head. No, most of my future plans involved me not being the center of any kind of attention. My stomach was about to implode. Public functions are not my thing. And to make matters worse, I kept thinking about how I had to talk in front of all these people after the parade.

We were starting to get to the part of Main that wasn't covered by trees, and I decided it was time to pull out the sunglasses rather than risk another squinty picture showing up in the newspaper. Which would happen because everyone had digital cameras out and flashing.

I leaned forward to get my sunglasses out of my purse, but I ended up leaning forward a bit too much and I slipped off the trunk and landed on my knees in the seat, half-crunching my purse.

Something cracked and I just knew it was my sunglasses.

I heard a guttural cry, but it wasn't me. DJ started yelling and grabbing for his gun. The governor started driving recklessly around the squad car in front, which immediately put on its siren. Patricia was screaming.

I looked up and Officer DeWeise was slumped over in the space I'd just vacated when I fell onto the seat, clutching his chest, eyes swinched tight. Blood was seeping around where his hands were on his chest.

I screamed. People all around us at the parade started screaming and running.

"Kate, get down and *stay down*!" DJ yelled at me. "Down to the floorboards, now!" He grabbed his radio while I scooted off the seat and onto the floorboard. DJ pushed Officer DeWeise onto the seat and then dove on top of him. "This is Officer Kirkpatrick! DeWeise has been shot. Repeat, DeWeise has been shot!"

The governor was still driving erratically. Patricia kept on screaming, covering her head with her hands.

I looked up at the pain-filled face of Officer DeWeise directly above me, one cheek smashed on the seat. "Are you okay?" I yelled. "Get to a hospital!"

The governor seemed stunned, scared, and started fumbling around, mashing the brake instead of the gas, and Officer DeWeise nearly fell on top of me. DJ braced himself against Patricia's headrest, so he didn't crush DeWeise.

"We need a driver!" DJ shouted into the radio.

The radio cracked something back and half a second later, someone was pushing the governor into the middle seat and was slamming the accelerator to the floor. The air whooshed around us, sirens blared, and I kept my hands knit together and my face down on the carpeted floorboards.

My heart was racing like crazy. I couldn't get a full breath in. Someone had been shot, and they'd been shot because I wasn't sitting where I was supposed to be sitting.

"No, no, no, no," I mumbled. "Oh no!"

"It's okay, Kate. It's okay," DJ said from where he was kneeling on the seat behind the prostrate Officer DeWeise. "Talk to me, DeWeise."

"Kid ..." he huffed, his eyes tightly closed in pain. "Are ... augh, are you okay?"

I was hyperventilating. "I'm okay," I managed.

"Kate, breathe. Breathe, Kate. In through the nose ..." DJ instructed. He scraped his knuckles down his cheek and just looked helplessly at me.

I squeezed my eyes shut and tried to concentrate on the breaths

I was taking. But really, all I could see when I closed my eyes was John X standing in the crowd aiming for me and shooting the funny Officer DeWeise instead.

"He's supposed to be in jail," I mumbled.

"He is," DJ said.

"Who did this then?" I looked up past DeWeise's tortured face and saw DJ's face get very hard.

He didn't answer me. We pulled to a stop and DJ hopped out over the window, and a second later they were helping Officer DeWeise out. He was gasping and moaning with every movement. Once he got out, I sat up on the floorboards.

There was bright red blood all over the shiny, velvet-white interior. It dripped down from the lid of trunk and was smeared on the backseat.

It should have been my blood.

Would have been, if I hadn't reached for my sunglasses right at that moment.

I couldn't help it.

I lurched out of the car.

And threw up.

Chapter Eleven

TWO HOURS LATER AND I WAS SITTING IN ONE OF THE hospital waiting rooms, clutching a crumpled Styrofoam cup that used to contain water in it.

Dad was pacing the floor in front of me, Mom was sitting beside me, arm around my shoulder.

I was staring at the crumpled cup.

What was Styrofoam anyway? Who made it? And was it really one of those materials that never decomposes and will be around after a nuclear explosion?

DJ and Detective Masterson were behind the big number 237 written on the door in front of us. That was Officer DeWeise's room. And last I'd heard, he was fine. The bullet had bounced off of his bulletproof vest but not before nicking him on the right side of his chest.

The doctor said he couldn't tell us any more because we weren't family or even friends. I told him that I was the person he took the bullet for, but the doctor didn't seem to care. And about thirty minutes ago, a sobbing woman ran down the hallway and burst into his room.

I was assuming a wife.

The press conference had been canceled. Now all the reporters were gathered outside the hospital. I was scared to leave.

Finally, DJ came out of the room.

"What happened? Is he okay?" I immediately asked.

DJ rubbed his face, looking ten years older this afternoon than he did this morning. "He's fine. His wife is here now. He got twenty-two stitches, but he should be back to normal within a couple of weeks. The doctor said that the force of the bullet cracked two of his ribs."

Detective Masterson came out then too. "We should let them be alone," he told DJ. Then he looked at me and my parents. "Come on, guys. We're taking you guys to the station," he said wearily.

I looked back down at the Styrofoam. Officer DeWeise had twenty-two stitches, two cracked ribs, and a sobbing wife.

Because of me.

Me and my dumb dream of being an artist.

I felt tears pooling in the corners of my eyes, but I tried my best to blink them away. Kate Carter never cried. That would be a sign of weakness, and Carters weren't weak.

Or so Dad said. Mom claimed that crying was good for the soul.

Dad nodded at the policeman. "Fine," he said crisply. I knew he was mad. He'd barely said a word after making sure I was okay when they got to the hospital. Just paced.

We stood and I gathered myself as I threw the crumpled cup away and followed DJ down the hospital corridor and to the front door.

Then I got scared. Someone had already tried to shoot at me once. What if he was out there waiting for me now? What if he was just around the other side of the huge grove of trees on the other side of the parking lot?

A throng of reporters were gathered outside the doors. Most were wearing suits, but there were a few who were dressed in jeans from the waist down and a collared shirt, tie, and sport coat from the waist up, like they'd been enjoying a nice day off before the parade happened.

DJ looked over at me. "Wait here with Detective Masterson," he

said. Then he made his way through the crowd of yelling reporters, jogged out to the parking lot, and pulled up right in front of
the door in the familiar black Tahoe.

We got inside as quickly as we could, pushing past a few reporters who kept yelling at me, asking me what I knew.

"Did you know he'd get shot, Kate?"

"Kate, why did you duck? Did you know the shooter was out
there?"

I wanted to tell them I wasn't ducking, I was trying to pre-
vent another squinty-eyed picture of me from showing up in the
newspaper. But Detective Masterson didn't give me any time to
respond. He half shoved me into the backseat of the Tahoe.

Everyone else clambered inside. My heart was racing.

Detective Masterson was sitting on one side of me, Mom on the
other. Dad rode in front with DJ.

The detective glanced over at me. "Kate?"

I took a deep breath and looked up at him. "Yeah?"

"Welcome to the life of a forensic sketch artist."

"Being shot at is part of the life of a forensic sketch artist?" I
asked.

He shrugged. "It can be. You're a member of the police force.
Police have to be prepared for anything."

"Apparently that's true even in a place like South Woodhaven
Falls," I said softly.

"Even in South Woodhaven Falls," the detective nodded.

We pulled up to the police station and DJ pushed me through
the doors and into the busy hum of the police station.

Deputy Slalom greeted us at the door and quickly ushered us
into his office.

He turned to us after the door closed, looking tired, old, and
defeated. He was wearing another business suit, but he now had
the jacket on the back of his chair, his sleeves rolled to his elbows
and his tie loose and hanging to one side.

"Well," he said, taking a deep breath. He looked at DJ and Detective Masterson. "What's the latest on DeWeise?"

"Doctor said two weeks recovery for the wound. Twenty-two stitches and two cracked ribs. He won't be in the field for a while, sir," Detective Masterson said.

"Especially if Mrs. DeWeise has anything to say about it," DJ said.

"Police work is hardest on the wife," Deputy Slalom said quietly, looking down at a picture frame on his desk. He shook his head slightly and looked up at Mom, Dad, and me.

"Kate, Mr. and Mrs. Carter, I'm very sorry you had to endure this today."

"Obviously, we now know what kind of danger Kate is in," Dad said darkly.

"Yes, sir. And preventative measures are going to be strictly enforced. Kate, when you go to school — "

"I'm sorry, what?" Dad interrupted loudly.

" — we will now have four officers around you at all times. Officer Kirkpatrick will continue to be your primary bodyguard."

"She is *not* going to school!" Dad burst, standing. "My daughter will not be going anywhere! She will stay home and will be constantly surrounded until we find whoever just fired a gun at her! Do you hear me?"

Deputy Slalom looked at Dad for a long moment. "Then John X just won."

"What?" Dad shouted.

"John X just won. Kate is no longer a free citizen of the United States and in a sense he put her in jail just like him. Oh, she might have a cushier couch to lounge on, but mark my words, Mr. Carter. John X will be thrilled to know that he has succeeded in stripping Kate of everything she took from him."

Dad sat down and covered his face with his hands. "She's my daughter," he said, quietly.

I'd never heard that tone in my dad's voice before. Particularly as it related to me.

More tears pooling in the corners of my eyes.

"I know that, sir. Believe me, I know that. I have a daughter too. And I don't envy the position you are in."

"So," Mom said, "you are saying that we should just continue on like today never happened."

"Absolutely not," Deputy Slalom said. "I'm saying that we should continue on as if today definitely happened. John X is mad. And because he's mad, one of his friends came out of the woodwork to the parade today. We weren't aware that John X had friends and I fear that if we don't find these people, we're looking at many more graveyard plots to be dug in the near future."

I really didn't like the term *graveyard plots* used in the same conversation that involved me.

It made me start thinking.

What did come after life? Was it really just a long nap like my dad thought? And if you never woke up again, was it technically considered a nap?

I'd asked my parents about heaven once. I was ten and the dog we had before Lolly had just died. So I'd asked if the dog had gone to heaven.

Dad told me heaven didn't exist. "It's a figment of some ancient writer's imagination," he'd told me. "And a nice idea. But honestly, I'd rather be sleeping than playing some little harp on a puffy white cloud for forever."

Mom had said that she thought heaven was more a state of mind than an eternal destiny. "I think that everyone goes to some kind of 'heaven,' if that's what you want to call it," she'd said, using her fingers for quotation marks. "But really I think you just remember your life after you die."

I'd always liked Mom's theory of heaven better than Dad's, because it was nice to think of our old dog just remembering all the fun days we'd had, but now I was wondering again.

Deputy Slalom was still talking. "It's your decision, Mr. Carter, but I would ask you to reconsider allowing Kate to attend school. Like I said, we will have four officers there at all times, plus Officer Kirkpatrick. I'm going to increase the amount of security at your house as well."

I raised my hand. "Does this mean I don't have to give a press release?" I asked.

The slightest hint of a smile crossed Deputy Slalom's mouth. "No, Kate," he said. "You don't have to give a press release."

"Good."

He looked back at Dad. "What do you think, Mr. Carter?"

Dad rubbed his face. "Your men protected her once already," he said, quietly. Which was Dad-speak for "I guess it's okay."

Deputy Slalom nodded. "Good." He looked at Detective Masterson. "I want you to be one of the ones constantly by Kate. And get Porter, Starr, and Klein. The four of you can be at the school too."

The detective nodded. "Will do, sir."

"Good." Deputy Slalom then looked at DJ. "Are you still up to this?" he asked him.

DJ nodded, chin set. "Yes, sir."

Deputy Slalom nodded. "Please rest assured that we have people working night and day on this case," he told us. "We will find out what's going on. Actually, there's a team from St. Louis coming up today to start working on this as well."

We finished talking and DJ stood. "Let's get you home," he said to me, but I think he was talking to my parents as well.

We rode home in silence. Dad was staring out the passenger window, Mom had her head leaned back against the headrest with her eyes closed, and Detective Masterson alternated looking out the window and looking at me.

A few reporters were outside my house when we pulled up, but DJ and the detective got us inside without too much trouble.

"Kate!" one lady kept yelling. "Kate!"

"No questions!" DJ snapped at her.

Lolly was wagging for us when we got inside.

"Hi, Lolly," I said, rubbing her silky black head. She wagged even harder and leaned against my leg, begging for more attention.

So I sat down on the sofa. Lolly put her drooly head in my lap and for once I didn't care. I turned on the TV and leaned back, trying to make myself relax.

The TV was tuned to the news channel, and they were showing footage of the parade that someone had caught on a personal camera. I watched it for a minute. There was me reaching for my sunglasses, there was Officer DeWeise clutching his chest and sagging sideways, and there was DJ yelling and pushing DeWeise on the backseat.

I shook my head slightly and changed the channel to something brainless. Ryan Seacrest was going on about Miley's new hairstyle and I left it on that channel, rubbing Lolly's head.

Someone had shot at me.

I closed my eyes, but all I could see was the blood dripping down the trunk of the governor's car and smearing on the pristinely white seat.

I kept my eyes open.

DJ sat down on the couch beside me. "Well," he said, looking at the TV. "This is definitely going to make me rethink getting those highlights I was thinking about."

I managed a smile at him.

He smiled back at me. "You have to stop thinking about it, Kate."

"Easier said than done, DJ."

He nodded. "Let's talk about something else then."

"Like what?"

He shrugged. "I don't know. We can talk about Miley's new hair color, but I'd kind of prefer if it was something other than that."

The detective came in from the kitchen then and sat on the rocker. "Long, long day," he said, stretching out, putting his feet on the ottoman. "What are you watching?"

"Miley's thinking of going blonde again," DJ told him.

"Oh," Detective Masterson hummed. "I think if I were her, I'd stay brunette. But then, what do I know about the fashions of dim-witted, psychologically stunted multibillionaires?"

"They brought in a renowned makeup artist to talk about it," DJ told him. "They think her skin tone isn't right for blonde. Apparently, you know more than you think you do."

The detective smiled proudly. "What can I say? I know lots about lots of things."

I knew they were bantering to get me to stop thinking about today.

It wasn't working very well.

"Does Officer DeWeise have any kids?" I asked.

DJ sighed and Detective Masterson answered me. "Yes, Kate. He's got two girls."

I nodded, picking at my cuticles, trying to swallow despite the huge gaping hole in my gut. "How old are they?" I asked quietly, trying to imagine what I would be thinking if my dad had been shot and was in the hospital.

"Nine and six." Then the detective straightened. "Kate, look at me."

I bit my lip and looked up at him.

"It's not your fault, Kate. Do you hear me?"

I nodded, but we both knew it was my fault. If I hadn't drawn John X, then those two girls wouldn't be scared for their dad tonight.

"Now," Detective Masterson said, "I want you to stop thinking about it and try to focus on something else."

"Do you believe in heaven?" I asked.

The detective didn't hesitate. "Yes, Kate, I do."

"What do you think it's like?" I remembered what Detective

Masterson told my dad about God. I was willing to bet that his view of heaven was a lot different than my parents'.

He took a deep breath. "I believe that heaven is where God resides, and it's where people who have trusted Jesus as their savior go after death."

Good solid churchy answer. "Do you think there are harps there?" I asked.

Detective Masterson grinned. "As in, are we playing them? No, I don't think we spend eternity playing harps. Or sitting on clouds. Or wearing diapers."

I wrinkled my nose at the last one. "What?"

"All those little angels sitting on a cloud playing harps and wearing a cloth diaper? Yeah, that's not a good view of heaven."

DJ had been very quiet through this whole conversation, so I turned and looked at him. "What do you think?" I asked him.

He shrugged. "I'm still trying to figure that out." Then he stopped talking and just watched the TV, where Ryan was now informing America that Usher was planning a new tour involving a few stops in Dallas, Austin, and Memphis.

"My mom thinks it's a subconscious thing and after we die, we just sort of remember and relive our previous life," I said.

Detective Masterson nodded. "I've heard that one before. So when does that end?"

"When does what end?"

"The remembering. When do you just stop having things to remember?"

I hadn't thought about that before. "I don't know."

We were all quiet for a minute. Now they were showing a music video of Usher. I decided that Usher was a fairly decent dancer.

I couldn't dance. My father was an engineer, so I had a good excuse. But still. I could never hope to have a future on *Dancing with the Stars*.

Not that I would want to wear any of the outfits they had to wear anyway. I have a thing about too many glittery sequins.

Mom and Dad had been talking in their room since we got home. I hadn't heard their door open, so I assumed they were still in there. Lolly still had her head planted squarely on my lap, and I was lazily drawing circles on the top of her head.

"So," I said.

"So," DJ parroted.

"School tomorrow." I looked at the detective. "You're coming too?"

He nodded and rocked in his chair. "Appears that way."

"I've got art first," I told him.

"Mm," he said, suddenly very interested in Usher's music video.

I looked at DJ, who just smiled at me. He leaned over a little closer. "I'll bet you ten bucks that he wears his blue polo shirt tomorrow," he whispered.

"What's with the blue polo?" I whispered back.

DJ opened his mouth to answer but got cut off. "I can hear you both, you do realize," Detective Masterson said grouchily.

"Okay. What's with the blue polo?" I asked him.

Detective Masterson glared at DJ. "I have no idea what you are talking about," he said, icily.

"He thinks he looks particularly nice in blue," DJ told me, no longer bothering to whisper.

I grinned. Especially when the detective blushed.

Bright red.

"I," he sputtered. "I do not think I look better in blue!"

"Sure you do," DJ said, easily. "It brings out your eyes, remember? Plus, if you wear navy, it's got the added bonus of being rather slimming as well, which we both know you need."

I was laughing by this point, and the detective picked up a throw pillow from the couch and chucked it at DJ, who ducked behind me. He didn't end up needing to duck — Detective Masterson had really lousy aim.

Mom and Dad walked out at that point. "What is going on here?" Mom asked, hands on her hips. "That pillow was a wedding gift. My great-aunt Charlotte crocheted that pillow. Are you pre-pared to replace it?" she lectured Detective Masterson.

He shook his head, instantly contrite. "No, ma'am. I'm sorry, ma'am."

"Good." She narrowed her eyes at DJ, who immediately stopped snickering.

"Sorry, ma'am."

"Thank you. You boys go wash up for dinner. And Kate? I could use your help."

I nodded and followed her into the kitchen while Detective Masterson and DJ went to wash their hands.

"Sheesh, all men are the same, Kate. They never grow up," Mom said, rinsing her hands in the kitchen sink. "Isn't that right, Dale?" she asked Dad.

Dad, who appeared to be in a better mood after having some time to cool off, nodded. "It's true, Kate. Marry wisely."

I wanted to remind my parents that I was sixteen and in no hurry to get married, but they continued on talking.

"Take Mike for example," Mom said, pulling a head of lettuce out of the fridge and handing it to me. "Mike is fairly mature for being a male, but he will probably never remember to call his wife when he's on his way home for dinner."

I thought that as long as Mike continued to exist as the Mike we all knew he probably would never get married. Maybe that's why my parents were already bringing up the *M*-word with me. They wanted grandkids.

Mom gave me a cutting board and a knife. "We're making taco salad. Chop the lettuce into small pieces," she said.

The police department had been giving Mom a grocery stipend for having DJ living with us. I imagine they'd increase it now that Detective Masterson was going to be here full-time as well.

I started chopping.

Dad sat at the kitchen table with the newspaper spread in front of him, since he didn't really get a chance to read it earlier today, what with church and all.

I sighed. It was still the same day that I'd seen Not-So-Silent Justin at South Woodhaven Falls First Baptist Church. It seemed like a long, long time ago.

"Look at this," Dad said, pointing to the sports section. Mom was busy browning two pounds of ground beef, and I was holding a sharp blade in my hand, so I was going to assume that he meant "listen to this."

And apparently he did mean that, because he started telling us about it. "There's some freshman kid at the high school who has started playing basketball and the guy is like six foot seven or something already." Dad shook his head and looked at me, whistling. "Can you imagine?"

"Yeah. That's Pete Somebody. He's only six foot seven?" I'd seen him in the hallways and always felt really bad for him. He looked like he'd rather be anywhere but surrounded by a school full of people who were mostly six feet and under. I tried not to stand by him. He made me feel abnormally short.

"I guess he's supposed to be really good. This says he scored thirty-one points and made seventeen free throws in the last game against one of Franklin County's high schools."

Sometimes I think Dad forgets that Mom and I were two girls who really didn't care too much for sports.

And by didn't care too much, I mean we were basically clueless. A free throw, to me, was something that you got at Peter Piper's Pizza in St. Louis at that ski ball game that I loved. Hit ten one-hundred-pointers in a row and you got a free throw. And a huge stack of tickets to redeem for cheap, made-in-China trinkets.

"Hmm," Mom said, stirring the meat. "That's neat, dear."

"What are we talking about?" DJ asked, coming into the kitchen and followed by Detective Masterson.

"Pete Walker, the six-foot-seven freshman at SWF High," Dad said, pointing out the article to them.

DJ nodded. "I heard about him. He's supposed to be really good. Especially at defense."

Dad looked so excited to have someone who cared about sports in the kitchen. The three of them started talking basketball and didn't finish until Mom and I were setting the bowls of chopped lettuce, steaming ground beef, diced tomatoes, onions, grated cheddar cheese, salsa, sour cream, and guacamole in front of them.

Mom brought over a bag of tortilla chips and we all sat down, pulling in an extra chair for Detective Masterson.

I looked around the table.

We'd gone from three people to five in a week. How much were we going to grow by next weekend?

Chapter Twelve

MONDAY MORNING AND THE CRISPIX WERE WINNING THE battle of sogginess.

I was tiredly fishing around for them in the bowl. I'd barely slept at all the night before, and when I did sleep, I kept seeing John X on the side of the street during the parade. He was holding a gun, and he kept laughing as he fired it. Then I'd see the blood-stain on the backseat of the convertible, only instead of Officer DeWeise getting hit, I would look down and see a big, round cannonball hole in my stomach. I would walk into the hospital and they would look at the huge hole in my stomach, just shake their heads, and hand me a pillow to try and shove into the gaping wound.

I'd wake up in a panic with my pillow clutched to my gut.

I chased another Crispix around in my bowl and caught it. It had no crunch left.

Yuck.

Dad looked over at me. "You understand that you are to go nowhere, I repeat *nowhere*, without the policemen. Is that understood?"

"Yes, sir," I yawned.

"And I'd prefer if you didn't even talk to anyone. Go to school, turn in your homework, do your classes, and come straight home. *Straight* home."

Suddenly, Dad had a fondness for stressed words, I guess. That and repeating things.

Mom came in, trying to put her earrings in. "Kate Carter, you listen to what your father says, and if you so much as even *think* something isn't right, you leave school right away with DJ and Detective Masterson. Agreed?" she asked sternly.

I nodded. "Agreed." Lots of italicized words in this house this morning.

"Good." She looked at the clock. "I have to run. You be safe at school." She kissed Dad good-bye and ran out the door, grabbing her briefcase as she went.

Dad and I left a few minutes later. DJ drove me to school in the black Tahoe. I rode in the backseat. I was going to forget how to drive if this kept up too much longer. I hadn't been behind the wheel since my drawing of John X had been flashed all over the news.

Detective Masterson was in the passenger seat and, yes, he was wearing the blue polo.

"Nice shirt," I told him as we pulled into the school parking lot. "Brings out your eyes."

Detective Masterson just glared darkly at DJ. "Thank you, Kate," he bit out.

DJ parked the Tahoe in the parking lot and then they walked with me into the school, one on each side of me. I was starting to feel like a prisoner. All I needed was one of those fashionable orange jumpsuits and an ankle-bracelet tracking device.

Art was up first and Miss Yeager was busy writing the assignment on the whiteboard when we walked in. She looked over and blushed a pretty shade of pink when she saw Detective Masterson.

"Oh, uh, hi!" she stumbled around.

The detective just smiled back at her, but there was a telltale flush to his face as well. I grinned over at DJ and then sat at my empty table.

DJ was much too punctual for Miss Yeager's class. No one

showed up in here until the bell was on its last chime over the intercom.

Not-So-Silent Justin came walking in right then and sat next to me at the table. He smiled at me but said nothing. Just pulled his sketchpad from his bag and found the pencils he'd rubber-banded together and sat there quietly at the table.

Okay, what was this?

I just looked at him. "Justin?" I said finally.

He looked back at me.

"You're doing it again."

He frowned.

"Not talking? Remember? I thought you were, like, stricken mute until we saw each other yesterday morning at church."

He made a noise deep in the back of his throat. "I'm not mute," he said, so quietly I had to lean forward to hear what he was saying.

"Then why don't you talk at school?" I asked.

He shrugged. "I don't have much to say here."

I just looked at him.

"But that does remind me, are you okay? I heard you had a rough afternoon," he said. He leaned forward. "Is the other cop okay?"

I nodded. DJ had talked to Officer DeWeise that morning and everything seemed to be healing as it was supposed to be. The hospital had even told him that if he continued feeling okay, he might be able to check out of the hospital tomorrow and finish recuperating at home.

"And you're okay?" Justin said.

"I'm fine," I said robotically, sort of like when I went to the doctor's office for my yearly checkup. Mom always said that I could have rubella and whooping cough, and I'd still croak out that I was fine.

Sometimes, it was better not to think about what was wrong. If you could forget, then everything would be okay again. So I was trying to forget yesterday.

DJ found an extra chair and sat down a couple of feet behind me while the detective stood in the back.

I felt like I was on display.

The bell rang and kids flooded into the art room. Allison Northing sat down next to me.

"Oh my *gosh*, Kate! You were *totally* shot at!" she screeched.

I winced from the decibel level she reached. That and the fact that I'd been trying to forget about it.

"It was *just* like one of those action movies my brother likes to watch!" Allison continued, oblivious to my pained expression, I guess.

"I'd rather not talk — " I started, but it was for no good. She kept on.

"There was a gun, someone got shot for you, you just *happened* to be reaching into the backseat. I mean ... *oh my gosh!*"

"Yeah, Allison, we could stop talking about — "

"I mean, someone was *shot* yesterday. Right next to you! I mean, the guy was probably aiming for *you*." She gasped. "Doesn't that, like, completely freak you out?"

I just looked at her, my gut twisting.

"Hey, I think we're starting, Allison," Justin said suddenly.

That shut her up completely. She stared at Justin, mouth open, eyes wide. He calmly turned and faced the front.

"All right, class!" Miss Yeager said loudly as everyone pulled out their sketchpads and pencils.

Allison elbowed me in the ribs. "Dude, did you *hear* that? Justin just spoke to me!"

"Allison?" Miss Yeager said, the warning in her voice.

Allison nodded.

"All right, I need everyone's menus from Friday and then we'll get started on today's lesson."

There was a loud rustling of papers as everyone dug their menus from their backpack. I'd finished mine on Saturday and I was very glad I had. There was no way I would have been able to concentrate on it last night.

Jailbird's Café looked like a rather charming place. There were pictures of men in striped black-and-white pajamas, carrying balls-and-chains, and lots of little touches like handcuffs around all the menu titles.

Miss Yeager gathered our menus and then turned to the white-board. She'd drawn a picture of the Froot Loops toucan on there.

"Anyone recognize this guy?" she asked.

"Toucan Sam," we all said dutifully.

"Very good. And welcome to another fascinating career in the art field, commercial art."

She continued to talk about how artists were paid to create characters such as Toucan Sam for different brands.

Again, I had trouble concentrating. I kept thinking about what Allison had said.

"The guy was probably aiming for you."

Miss Yeager was talking and drawing the Trix rabbit on the board, but I didn't hear a word of what she was saying.

Aiming for you.

The day passed by very slowly. Everyone I passed in the hallway was taking care to walk at least thirty feet away from me. I felt like I'd been diagnosed with scurvy or something. No longer were people yelling out my name in adoration.

Now they whispered it as I passed.

"There's Kate Carter," I heard one guy hiss to another. "She got shot at yesterday. Put a cop in the hospital."

I tried to just stare straight ahead and I tried even harder to not listen, but it was hard when the halls became so quiet I heard the rattling of people's teeth against their orthodontia whenever I stepped outside the classroom.

DJ and the detective were never more than a few inches away, but it didn't make me feel any less alone. Even Maddy wasn't at school today. She'd texted me this morning saying she'd woken up with white patches on her tonsils, and her mother was making her go to the doctor before she had to get her throat amputated.

I texted back that she probably just had tonsillitis, and people lived from that every day without the threat of amputation. But Maddy's mom is something of a hypochondriac, and any time Maddy got even a case of the sniffles, she was immediately marched to the doctor in case it was something serious like the German measles instead of the common cold.

Sometimes I wondered if being a hypochondriac made you more susceptible to diseases. Everyone I knew who was constantly freaking out about getting sick and rubbing their hands with that sticky goopy stuff was always getting sick. So either the goopy stuff wasn't working or their immune systems were so overprotected that they weren't even sure what to do with a germ anymore.

We drove home from school in silence. Detective Masterson kept looking in the rearview mirror at me with a worried look on his face. DJ kept clearing his throat like he was going to say something, and then he'd stop before he did.

Detective Masterson finally spoke as we turned the corner onto my street.

"You okay, Kate?"

"I'm fine." There it was again.

"You seem kind of..." He let his voice trail off and shrugged as he parked in my driveway. For once, there weren't any reporters around.

I felt a huge wave of relief crash over my shoulders at that fact.

"I'm fine," I said again. "I'm just tired."

"You definitely didn't sleep very well," Detective Masterson said. He turned in his seat and looked at me. "Nightmares?"

I hated having to leave my door open at night. This was getting embarrassing.

I shrugged, which was my way of saying, "Yes, but I don't want to talk about it." I guess he picked up on the clue, because he unbuckled and hopped out of the car, opening the back door for me.

"You've got lots of homework," DJ said. "I'd forgotten how much homework high school teachers give."

"Keeps kids off the streets," Detective Masterson said as we walked inside.

The detective was going to be one of those fathers who tried to give his kids more homework than was needed just so they were doing something productive. I know this because my dad has said many times that if teachers were stricter with homework, we'd have far fewer juvenile delinquents in prison these days.

I'd felt the need to point out that the definition of juvenile delinquent was someone who just didn't care regardless, and if they didn't care when there was less homework, what made Dad think that they would care if there was more?

Which is when Dad had pulled out a stack of his college math textbooks for me in case I ever got bored.

I tried very hard to look busy around Dad most of the time.

I took my books to the kitchen table and tried to focus on my algebra homework. We were learning about how x and imaginary numbers worked together.

I hated math. Was I ever going to use imaginary numbers in any career I picked? No. There was zero point to me learning this.

"How's it going?" DJ asked, walking into the kitchen a minute later.

I shrugged. I was in the middle of finding x and it was just better if I did it robotically instead of thinking too much about that sentence.

"Finding X" had too many other meanings for me right now.

"I just got off the phone with Officer DeWeise," DJ said.

I looked up at him. "Is he okay?"

DJ nodded. "He'll be fine. The doctors told him that everything is looking really good."

I breathed a sigh of relief. "Good."

"Yep." He pulled a pear from the fridge and started cutting it into slices.

I looked back down at the page in my math book that I was working on.

Find X *in the following problems.*

I slammed the book shut.

Tuesday and Wednesday passed by like they were on repeat from Monday. I went to school, everyone pointed and whispered about me in the hallway, I turned in homework, Miss Yeager and Detective Masterson blushed at each other but didn't talk, and Justin said "hi" twice and that was it.

Every night, I'd watched the news and every night, Ted Deffle at KCL would tell some new shocking story about John X's life before prison. New people who knew him were coming forward and all of them couldn't believe he was a serial killer.

"Why, I would have left my kids with him while I ran to the grocery store for milk," one lady from Franklin county said on Wednesday night's news.

Detective Masterson had said that the police there should just go ahead and write her info down because she was likely going to be calling in a missing child's report sometime in the near future.

Thursday didn't start that much differently.

The school again went painfully quiet when I walked in the doors. I hadn't decided if it was because they were worried about being shot if they got into near proximity of me or if it was the two very obvious, despite their attempts at plain clothes, cops next to me.

Maddy, though, was back on Thursday.

She came hustling over, shoving her backpack onto one shoulder. "Kate, I'm so glad you're here," she whispered.

"What's with all the whispering?" I asked. "How come no one is talking in a normal-toned voice anymore?"

She gave me a *duh* look. "Because. No one wants to get shot."

I sighed.

"Anyway, I'm glad you're here. I was talking to Tyler and he said that he heard that John X had a cousin named Bridget who goes to this school."

Detective Masterson and DJ exchanged a look, and I saw the detective pull his phone from his pocket and start texting someone.

"Wait — Tyler?" I asked.

She nodded.

"As in the same Tyler who broke your heart all of a week ago?"

"We're back together," she announced, flashing a big smile. "He apologized. He said that he was totally in the wrong, and he never meant to hurt me."

Fabulous. I managed a smile. "Great, Maddy. That's great." I wished I could have been more excited, but now I simply got to watch the dramatic breakup again sometime in the future. Tyler really was a big jerk. I never could see what made Maddy so in love with him. He treated her like garbage.

"Thanks!" she said all perkily. We passed by a group of football players who were gathered in the hall, and Tyler immediately came over.

"Oh, hi, Kate," he said, slinging his arm around Maddy. "And you guys must be the undercover cops." His voice dropped a couple of decibel levels. "Do you really think someone will try to shoot Kate here?"

A real winner, that Tyler. Always had the nicest thing to say and the most perfect time to say it.

Detective Masterson frowned at Tyler — he didn't even bother answering him. We stopped outside the art classroom.

"Well. Anyway. See you later, Kate."

Tyler left and Maddy rolled her eyes. "I don't know why he asked that." She looked at the policemen. "He's really not that callous most of the time."

Oh, he really was. But I didn't say anything.

"So, Kate, can I come study with you afterwards today?"

I nodded. "Sure." Honestly, I'd missed Maddy's incessant chatting over the noise of Ryan Seacrest while I was trying to do my homework. "How are the tonsils?"

She waved her hand. "Oh, they're fine. The doctor said that I'd probably have to get them out sometime this year, but I'm going to wait until summer to do it so I don't have to miss a bunch of school. He said that I probably should have had them out when I was a kid. Want to see them?"

I winced. "No, thanks." Looking in people's mouths was not a favorite pastime of mine. Dentistry was out as far as a future career choice.

She nodded. "All right then. I'll see you after school. Bye!" She waved and left, running down the hall to make her first class on time.

"Charming friend," Detective Masterson said under his breath.

"Equally charming boyfriend." DJ nodded.

"Hey," I said. "Maddy is my best friend, so please be nice to her."

Detective Masterson shrugged. "I'll be nice."

We pushed through the door to art class, and there were only six other people in there as the bell rang. I frowned and looked back into the hallway. Usually, there are around fifteen more kids in my class.

Miss Yeager turned from the board and looked at all of us. "Good morning, everyone," she said.

I sat down next to Justin and Allison and looked around. I raised my hand.

"Yes, Kate?"

"Where is everyone today?"

Miss Yeager tried to hide a wince in my direction, but then I understood.

"Oh," I said, shaking my head slightly. "I get it. Never mind."

Allison elbowed me in the ribcage. "I heard that all these moms had this meeting last night because they think that it puts all their kids in danger for you to be here, and so they pulled all their kids out of school," she whispered.

"Allison!" Miss Yeager said sharply. "Now is not the time."

She shrugged at Miss Yeager and then pulled her pencils out of her backpack, looking at me. "I'm just saying what I heard."

I sat there quietly in my chair, facing the whiteboard and trying not to look around at all the empty seats. The moms panicked? They had a meeting? I was preventing fourteen kids from coming to school today?

This was getting to be too much. Didn't they realize that's why Detective Masterson and DJ were here?

Miss Yeager sent an apologetic look my direction and started the lesson. It was just a review, so I started to drift off in the midst of it.

My stomach was cramping. I'd always been the girl that no one even noticed, and now, everyone noticed me. Everyone was scared to stand close to me.

I felt like a walking time bomb.

Miss Yeager finished class right as the bell rang. "Kate, hold on a minute please," she said over the clanging. The rest of the class gathered their stuff and left.

Justin sent me a half-smile as he packed his backpack. "Chin up," he whispered, and then left.

Miss Yeager came over and sat down in Allison's vacated chair. "You are not the cause of this," she said.

"Come on, Miss Yeager," I said. I was so tired of people telling me this was not my fault. It was my fault. If I hadn't drawn John X, then I never would have caused Officer DeWeise to get shot or have part of the school staying home out of fear.

"Kate, people get scared over situations that they don't need to be scared about," Miss Yeager said.

I just sighed at her and the two policemen standing next to us. "They don't need to be scared about this? I've got two cops following me around like I'm the President's daughter, I've gotten a cop with a wife and two kids shot and put in the hospital, I can't sleep at night because of the nightmares, and my mother has stopped buying me Crispix because she saw me tracing the *x* in the title yesterday." I let my breath out.

Miss Yeager reached over and rubbed my shoulder. "I'm so sorry, Kate. This is all because of me and a stupid idea I had. I'm so sorry."

"If it's any consolation," Detective Masterson said, "people still think you're a hero, Kate. Those people who were waiting for vindication for the women who died have gotten it. And John X will never be released from prison."

"Apparently, he doesn't need to be, and people still get shot," I said bitterly. I slammed my hands down on the table. "You know what? I think I'm going to go home for the rest of today."

I stood, grabbed my backpack, and left. Detective Masterson and DJ hurried to keep up with me as I marched out of the school and to the black Tahoe.

"Kate. Kate, slow down," DJ said, grabbing my forearm. "Are you sure you don't want to stay for the rest of the day?"

"What's the point? So I can see all the rest of the empty tables at school? No thanks. Everyone wishes I would just stay home anyway."

Detective Masterson unlocked the Tahoe, and I climbed in. It was a quiet drive home.

DJ parked in the driveway, and we walked to the front porch. There sat three more bouquets on the front porch. I was willing to bet that at least one was from the news crew at KCL who was still begging for an interview. We each grabbed one and went inside.

I set my bouquet on the kitchen counter next to the other two. They were pretty. Daisies, roses, tulips … it looked like a funeral had happened in our house, because these were everywhere.

I was beginning to hate the smell of flowers.

I yanked the notes from the bouquets.

Dear Kate, thank you for your selfless contribution to society …

Kate, we are so grateful for such patriots in America …

Dear Kate, if you could please call our newsroom at 555 – 3422, we'd love to have you on our show …

The last one was from KCL. The first two were signed from Phyllis in St. Louis and the Kleins in Springfield, Missouri.

I put all the notes in the teetering stack of notecards on the kitchen counter and left the flowers where they were. One thing was sure — South Woodhaven Falls florists had been reaping the benefit from my actions.

They were about the only ones who were.

It was only ten o'clock in the morning, and I had no idea what to do with the rest of the day. I didn't have any homework, since I'd skipped out on classes. Mom and Dad were both at work for the remainder of the day.

It was just me and the cops.

Two men and a high school dropout.

Wasn't that the name of a movie?

I wondered if skipping school today classified me as a juvenile delinquent. I'd have to ask Dad later tonight.

"So," DJ said, joining me in the kitchen. "What do you want to do for the rest of today?"

I shrugged. "I don't know." Usually, when I was completely bored, I would go to my room and draw for hours.

I was starting to hate drawing. Anytime I sat down to sketch, the only face I saw was John X's.

Detective Masterson came into the kitchen, holding his cell phone. "Guess what?" he said, though I wasn't sure if it was directed to me or DJ.

Judging by DJ's lack of a response, he didn't know whom the question was for either.

Detective Masterson didn't bother to wait for one of us to answer. "There was a witness at the parade."

DJ immediately straightened. "Witness? Someone saw the shooter?"

"Apparently, they saw them clear as day. They've just been too scared to come forward with that information."

They both exchanged a look for a minute and then both turned to me. I was fishing in the pantry for the stash of M&M's Dad and I had hid weeks ago. I could feel their stares on my back.

I winced. "No," I said, knowing what was coming.

"Kate," Detective Masterson started.

I found the bag of M&M's and tore into it. "I don't want to. Have the real artist guy do it."

Detective Masterson let out a single, staccato laugh. "Ha! Like that would help us at all. Larry's sketches have only gotten us leads for nice old ladies buying their grandbabies teething rings. We've never caught the person we were looking for off of Larry's sketches."

"Seems like it's time to hire a new sketch artist then," I said, popping a handful of M&M's into my mouth. "And one who's legal to vote," I said around the colored globs of chocolate, since both of them opened their mouths at the same time.

"Kate," DJ said again. "If we find this guy, maybe we can get him to talk. We can find out if there are more people after you. We can find out how many more friends John X has."

I chewed in silence, looking at them and then at the floral shop in my house. Then I thought about Officer DeWeise and his two kids waiting at home for their daddy. And how my dad's voice cracked when he was talking about me staying protected.

It made sense. If we caught the guy who shot at me during the parade, maybe he was the last of my worries. Maybe he was John X's only friend, and maybe if they were stuck in prison together they'd only get to reminisce about the good old days of killing innocent women instead of continuing to do it.

Maybe.

I looked again at the flowers decorating our entire house. From the kitchen, I could count at least twenty-two bouquets scattered around our house. That didn't count the handful that were upstairs. Mom said we were going to need to start giving them out to the neighbors.

About half of them were from KCL, but the other half were all families and couples and women who had written some really sweet thank-you cards.

I was scared to leave my house for fear of John X, one woman had written. *Thank you for giving me my freedom back.*

Now if only I could find a bit of that freedom as well.

I sighed and swallowed and looked at the two policemen in front of me.

"Fine." I said it quietly, but both of them reacted like a firework had exploded.

"Great!" Detective Masterson said, doing a fabulous impression of Tony the Tiger. "I'll call Deputy Slalom right now." He immediately left, dialing as he went.

"Awesome," DJ said, patting my shoulder. "I knew we could count on you, Kate."

Detective Masterson appeared back in the kitchen seconds later. "We're going to the station right now," he said. "Think you should call your parents? Don't forget the code we talked about."

I nodded. I picked up our house phone and dialed my mom's work first.

"Hello, Claire Carter's office." Madge, Mom's ancient secretary, answered the phone.

"Hi, it's Kate."

"One moment."

A second later, my mom answered. "Kate? Honey, is everything okay?"

"Just wanted to be sure you remembered my dentist appointment was today," I told her, nodding at the policemen. We weren't supposed to say exactly where we were going, just in case.

I felt like I was in one of those spy movies.

Only I felt like I should be cooler. I felt a little like Steve Carell's character in *Get Smart*. Kind of goofy.

Mom cleared her throat. "Okay, honey. Thanks for reminding me."

So now Mom knew that I was not at school, I was going to the police station, and everything was fine.

"Okay. Bye, Mom."

"Love you, Katie-Kin."

I paused, holding the phone with both hands. "I love you too, Mom."

Dad didn't take it quite as easily. "The dentist?" he repeated. "Why in the world are you going to the dentist right now? Shouldn't you be in school?"

He either didn't remember the code or was trying to find out why I was going to the police station, but we hadn't discussed the code past the dentist part.

"Well, I, uh, have a cavity, I think," I said, around a mouthful of M&M's. "It's kind of painful, so I called the dentist. They said to come on over, and they'd take a look at it. It's pretty urgent, Dad."

Then it clicked.

"Oh," Dad said, suddenly. "Right. Well, then you should probably go in."

"Yep. I'm on my way there."

"Okay. Well. Buckle your seatbelt." *Bring the cops.*

"Always, Dad. Love you."

"Love you back."

I nodded to DJ and Detective Masterson. "Okay. Let's go."

Chapter Thirteen

I FOUND IT KIND OF SAD THAT THE POLICE STATION LOOKED so familiar. Same desks, same cubicles. Same feeling of being in an office hawking paper supplies instead of a place dedicated to upholding the law.

Deputy Slalom was waiting for us when we got there. He was wearing his typical outfit of a button-down, long-sleeve shirt and a tie. This time, he was still wearing his jacket.

Must have been a slow day.

"Hi, Kate," Deputy Slalom said, holding open the door to one of the conference rooms. "Glad you were able to come."

I'd never heard a policeman excited about a high school student skipping classes, but things have been a little weird lately.

I nodded. "I brought my pencils," I said, holding up a handful of pencils rubber-banded together. I didn't bring my sketchpad. I figured surely the police station had paper.

Then again, with all the city and county budget cuts that have been happening constantly, maybe that wasn't a good assumption.

Deputy Slalom showed me into the conference room and DJ followed me. Detective Masterson went to go check his office.

There was a huge sketchpad set up on an easel in the room, as well as a couple of chairs, two tables, a box of facial tissues, a huge binder, and a water dispenser.

I'd never drawn on an easel before. Miss Yeager didn't have the money to buy easels for everyone in art class, so we got to draw on the table. And at home, I always drew on my desk.

I've heard it's better for your wrist if you use an easel, but since I've never practiced on one, I'm not sure if I could draw as well.

"Make yourself comfortable," Deputy Slalom said to me. He patted DJ on the shoulder. "And feel free to take a break, if you want. I'm going to hang out in here for a few minutes."

DJ nodded and looked at me. "You okay?" he asked.

"Go take a break," I said, filling a paper cup with water. "I'm fine."

DJ left.

Deputy Slalom nodded to the chair next to the easel. "The witness is on her way in. Let me explain a little about how this works."

I sat down and took the rubber band off my pencils. Deputy Slalom sat in the chair opposite me.

"We don't give out the witness's last name," he started. "But this woman's first name is Carol. She was at the parade with her three kids when she saw the shooting."

"How old is she?" I asked.

"Probably forty. Maybe forty-five. With all these new creams women are putting on their faces, it's getting harder to tell." Deputy Slalom nodded to the huge binder. "In that book are nearly a thousand different facial components. Everything from noses, ears, and moles. Our former sketch artist liked to use it to try and draw out the memory from the witness."

Former sketch artist. I sighed. Poor Larry.

I picked up the heavy binder and flipped through about ten pages of eyebrows before even I was confused at what I was looking at. They started looking more and more like dead centipedes.

If I were asked to describe someone after looking at one thousand different facial features, I don't think I'd even be able to accurately describe my mother, much less someone I'd seen for barely a minute.

No wonder Larry's sketches always came out wrong.

"Do I have to use this?" I asked, closing the binder.

Deputy Slalom shook his head. "You can do whatever you want to. Normally, I wouldn't give that much freedom to an artist, but considering how much that sketch of John X was picture quality, who am I to judge your methods?"

There was a rap on the door and a policeman I hadn't met stuck his head in. "She's here, boss."

"Send her in," Deputy Slalom said, standing.

A short woman with cropped brown hair walked in, clutching her purse nervously. She didn't wear a lot of makeup, just some eyeliner and mascara as far as I could tell. Her cheeks were flushed though.

I was hoping it was from the nerves and not the flu. Getting sick right now wasn't a high priority for me.

"Hi, Carol. Thank you for coming in," Deputy Slalom said in a nice, soothing voice. He ushered her in and had her sit in the chair opposite me.

She just stared at me. "You're okay?" she said quietly, in a sweet Southern accent.

I nodded. "I'm okay."

"And the policeman who was shot?"

I looked at Deputy Slalom, imagining he had the more up-to-date information.

"He was discharged today," he said. "A couple of cracked ribs and a few stitches. You have to love bulletproof vests," he said, lightly. I knew he was trying to lessen Carol's anxiety, but I think just the sight of me was enough to send her back into a fit.

She only nodded.

"Carol, Kate here is going to draw what you remember. Okay? You two take as much time as you need, and let us know if we can get you anything."

Deputy Slalom's secretary brought in a plate full of cookies, brownies, and fruit then. "Here you go, ladies," she said, setting it on the table in between us.

Deputy Slalom looked at me. "You good?"

I nodded.

"Okay. Let me know if you need anything. I'll send Kent in here in a minute."

He left.

The room was very quiet. Carol was alternating between staring at me, the easel, and the plate of food.

I was trying to figure out what to do next.

"So, uh," I started strongly, just like my speech teacher loved. "Um, what do you do?"

Carol blinked and looked away from the cookies and up to my face. "I'm sorry, what?"

"What do you do for a job?"

"I'm a stay-at-home mom."

I nodded. "That's neat." Evidently, her daughters don't have to worry about going on imaginary adventures like that story about the little kid who was home too much by herself. "How old are your kids?"

She took a deep breath, relaxing her iron grip on her purse slightly. "Nine, seven, and four. The older two are at school right now. The baby is with my husband." She dug into her purse and pulled out a wallet-sized photo. There was a huge Christmas tree in the background and a bunch of little blonde girls, a blond man, and Carol in the picture.

"Aw, they are cute," I said, taking the picture and staring at it for the appropriate amount of time before handing it back.

"Thanks." She managed a small smile at me. "If you don't mind me asking, how old are you?"

"Sixteen," I said.

"Wow," she breathed. "You are young."

There are only a few statements that put a complete end to a conversation, but that is one of them. What was I supposed to say to that? Yes, I am? No, not really?

I cleared my throat. "So, um, I'm actually not sure why they wanted me to come draw for you, but I'm trying to do anything I can to help this investigation," I said.

She nodded. "I'm sorry it took me so long to come forward. My girls ..." She looked away and shook her head. "Well. You understand."

I didn't, but I nodded like I did. "Did your girls ..." I winced. "Did they see ...?"

She shook her head immediately. "No, they were with their father. I was trying to find the stand with those corn dogs."

Oh, the corn dogs. Which I hadn't tasted.

"Anyway, I couldn't find the stand and I was over on the side of the street, and there were a bunch of people cheering for you, so I walked over to get a better look at you."

"Did you ever get one?" I asked.

She shrugged. "There was a tall man in front of me, so I kind of caught a side profile of you."

I shook my head. "No, I meant, did you ever get a corn dog?"

A tiny smile crossed her face. "No. The parade was canceled."

"Sorry about that."

"Me too."

She looked more at ease. She even set her purse on the floor instead of clutching it tightly in her lap.

I arched my back in the uncomfortable, hard plastic chair. I wasn't sure what to do at this point. When I sketched John X, Miss Yeager just read me a long description of what he looked like. I didn't have to do the probing thing.

It felt weird asking a woman I barely knew a million questions, though. Sort of rude, even.

"What are your daughter's names?" I asked, just trying to get to know her better.

"Meghan, Rachel, and Elise," she said.

"Pretty." I smiled.

"Do you have any siblings, Kate?"

I nodded. "I have a brother. He's not around very much. He's in college in California. He's going to be an engineer, so he can't take very much time off school." I shrug. "We don't talk much."

She nodded, knowingly. "I have a brother like that. He lives in Maine and we never talk unless I'm in labor."

"You had a long stretch of not talking then, between your second and third girl," I said. "Is he an engineer too?"

She laughed. "No, he's working as a technical support something or another. He's in charge of a bunch of wires, basically."

"Do you want a cookie?" I asked, pointing to the tray. I wasn't starving, but breakfast had been early morning and it was nearing eleven thirty. Almost lunchtime. I pulled a chocolate chip cookie off the plate and Carol picked a brownie.

"I really don't need this," she fretted, rubbing a hand on her hip.

I tried very hard not to roll my eyes. All adult women are the exact same. I was just thrilled that there was real — or fake, according to my mother — sugar in the cookies. I hadn't had a real chocolate chip cookie for far too long.

"Careful," Carol said, smiling at me. "You'll worry about it too."

Apparently I wasn't as good at hiding the eye roll as I thought I was.

We talked about nothing and everything for the next thirty minutes. She grew up in Arkansas, which explained the accent, married her husband in Georgia, and then moved to South Woodhaven Falls when her husband got a job in the St. Louis outskirts.

"I hate that he commutes so far to work every day, but I love living in a small town," she said. "It's so good for the girls."

We finally got back around to the parade after noon.

"I guess I first noticed him because he was wearing a hooded sweatshirt and had the hood on," she said, pulling a pineapple chunk from the tray. "And it was very sunny, you remember. And warm. You definitely did not need a hood on."

I looked away from Carol nibbling on the pineapple so I could start imagining the man.

"He wasn't very tall," she continued. "He was probably close to Steve's height." Steve was Carol's husband. She'd already told me he was five-eight and therefore had solidified their daughters' shortness forever.

"And he was wearing sunglasses," she said. "Those kind that look like something Tom Cruise would wear in *Top Gun*. Wait, is that too old of a reference for you?"

I grinned. "My mom loves *Top Gun*."

"Meg Ryan was adorable in that movie."

I nodded.

She talked for the next hour and I listened carefully. The man she'd seen had what looked like short brown hair under the hood, the aviator sunglasses, a five o'clock shadow, and a sharp chin. She hadn't seen his ears, but he had nice cheekbones.

"He was probably around thirty, I'd guess," she said.

I still hadn't drawn anything. There was no point to drawing something I'd only have to erase later.

"How about his nose? His lips? Is Elise excited to start kindergarten?" I prodded her with questions about the man and about her family whenever she stopped talking.

Detective Masterson came in and out during the meeting, and when he came in at one, he brought hamburgers.

At two, I picked up my pencil and pulled the sketchpad off the easel. Carol was still talking about how she'd kind of thought something shifty was going on with the man.

"He kept looking back and forth and back and forth," she said. "And he kept both of his hands in the front pockets of his sweatshirt. Like I said, it was much too warm to be wearing something like that."

I started drawing. I closed my eyes and saw the face of the man she had described. But it's not just physical description that mattered. There were indefinable qualities that played into how someone looked. How they acted, what they lived through.

I worked on the sketch for almost an hour. Carol would lean over and look at it and make a few comments.

"His nose was a little more straight," she said.

I fixed the nose and kept working.

"Kate?" she asked about thirty minutes later when I took a break to stretch.

"Yeah?"

She fidgeted and I braced for a hard question. "Why did you lean forward?" she asked quietly.

The question of the week.

I put my pencil down. "I don't know," I said, truthfully. "I needed my sunglasses, so I leaned forward to get them because my purse was in the backseat. But I have no idea why it was exactly at that time."

She looked at me and nodded. "Okay."

I picked up my pencil and looked at my half-finished sketch. The man's forehead and eyes were done, his nose was coming along.

"Carol?" I asked.

"Yes, Kate?"

I set the pencil back down. "Do you believe in God?"

She pursed her lips, eyes going a little bit dark. She didn't answer me for a long minute, and then she let out her breath. "I don't know, honestly."

I nodded. "Okay."

"You think that's the reason you leaned forward right then?"

I shrugged. "Well. I don't know. I mean, if I hadn't, I would have been shot. And I wasn't wearing a bulletproof vest, so the odds are good that I could have died. So, for me to bend over at exactly that time ..."

I let my voice trail off, and I picked up my pencil again.

Carol didn't say anything.

It took me another forty-five minutes before I finished the drawing. We didn't talk as much during the last part of it.

I held it up when I finished. "What do you think?" I asked quietly.

She looked at the drawing and then closed her eyes. "That's him."

Detective Masterson walked in.

"How are we doing, girls?" he asked.

Carol picked up her purse. "That's him," she said, pointing. "That's him and it's time for me to go." She looked over at me as she stood. "Thank you, Kate. Stay safe."

She left.

I looked at the drawing. A man in his early thirties wearing a hood and aviator glasses looked back at me.

"Think it will help?" I asked Detective Masterson.

He picked up the pad. "I think you are a very talented artist. And beyond that, you have a natural affinity toward forensic sketching, Kate."

I shook my head. "I doubt it. I didn't have a clue what I was doing."

"You put the witness at ease, you asked questions that went beyond the description, and you really made her feel comfortable enough to tell you what she saw." Detective Masterson was smiling proudly at me. "I think you did great."

I smiled.

I stretched my hands out in front of me, popping my knuckles. My fingers were sore, but my headache was worse. I chugged another cup of water and stood, stretching.

"Well, how did it go?" Deputy Slalom asked, walking in.

"She did great, sir. Here's the sketch." Detective Masterson handed the pad to the deputy.

Deputy Slalom took it and studied it for a minute, eyes narrowed. "Hmm," he said. "Send this to all the news networks and let's get some flyers made. I want the hermit who lives four counties over to know what this guy looks like. Got it?"

Detective Masterson grinned at me. "Yes, sir."

Chapter Fourteen

THE SKETCH WAS ON THE FIVE O'CLOCK NEWS WHEN WE got back to my house. Mom had apparently just gotten home; her car was making those weird popping and hissing sounds like when you first turn the engine off. Dad still wasn't there yet.

She was sitting in the living room watching Ted Deffle on KCL when DJ, Detective Masterson, and I walked in.

The picture I drew was plastered on the TV. Mom looked over at me from the sofa.

"Your work?" she asked.

I nodded and sat next to her. She put her arm around me.

Ted was talking. "This is the description of a man thought to be the shooter at last Sunday's parade, which left a member of our fine police force in the hospital. If you recognize this man, please call the hotline number listed on the screen. All calls are considered anonymous."

The picture changed back to Ted's fake-sun-tanned face. "In other news, people are still talking about the devastating events that occurred at the May Day parade ..."

"So," Mom said, turning Ted to mute. "You skipped school and went to 'the dentist.'" She looked at DJ and Detective Masterson, then back to me. "Your idea or theirs?"

"Mine," I said. "The skipping school part, at least."

"Uh-huh. Remember last year when you caught mono? You

refused to stay home and sleep? I basically had to tie you down in bed because you were so worried about missing school." She looked at me in the eyes. "Today doesn't sound like you."

"Does anything that's happened in the last week sound normal?" I asked. "Other kids' parents are flipping out about their kids' safety now. There was like a third of school who wasn't there today, thanks to me."

Mom sighed. "So, you left."

"Maybe it's better if I just stay here for a while. Maddy can bring me my homework and I'll keep up with everything here." I gasped. "Maddy!" She was supposed to come over today after school and I totally forgot about it.

I don't have a cell phone. What if she waited on my front porch for an hour before finally giving up? Or worse, what if a news crew was here and they made her give an interview?

Or much worse . . .

I shut my eyes, not wanting to think about *that* scenario.

"She left a message saying she wasn't going to be able to come over today after all," Mom said, patting my arm. Then she looked at me wryly. "She had a dentist appointment."

Detective Masterson started laughing. DJ smiled.

Mom just smiled and sighed. "Your father is on his way home, so I'm going to go start making dinner. We can talk about the you-staying-home-from-school idea when he gets home." She ran her hand through the back of my hair, like she used to when I was a little kid, before she stood and left the room.

Detective Masterson sat down in the recliner. "So, no more school for you?" he asked.

I sighed. "What if the other kids' parents are right and I'm just a big bull's-eye to all of them?"

The muted TV was flashing the picture I'd just drawn again, along with the hotline number.

"How many calls do you guys usually get on stuff like this?" I asked.

DJ sat on the opposite end of the couch from me and sighed, looking over at Detective Masterson. "Um … maybe a good two hundred? Three hundred depending on how publicized the case is." He shrugged. "Most of them are from people who swear they saw that man in front of them in the grocery store."

"Do you go check all of them out?"

Detective Masterson nodded. "Unless they are completely ridiculous, then yes, we do."

It seemed like a lot of busywork to me, but I didn't say anything. Instead, I reached for the phone, because I needed to tell Maddy to get my homework for me.

She answered her cell phone on the second ring. "Well, if it isn't Kate Escape," she said, and I could hear the grin in her voice.

"What?" I asked.

"Kate Escape. It's what everyone at school is calling you since you left this morning. Personally, I think it's kind of catchy." She sighed. "Wish I'd come up with it."

Fabulous. Now I'm a juvenile delinquent and I have a trendy new nickname. Dad was going to make me memorize his calculus books for fear that I'm morphing into the next resident at the juvy hall near here.

"Clever," I said.

"So, why'd you leave, Kate?"

"Everyone is scared when I get there. All the parents are rioting. It's better for me to just stay home."

"Oh, yeah, I heard about the parent thing. They asked my dad if he was going to go."

"Did he?"

"Kate, considering he didn't even make it to my junior high graduation, what do you think?"

True. Bad question to ask. Maddy's parents tend to use stuff to make up for their lack of affection. They missed junior high graduation and gave her the complete set of *Friends* DVDs. Her shiny brand-new Tahoe? She had been asking them for weeks to try and make it to the huge school debate that she was in, and both her mom and dad had promised to be there. Then they didn't show.

So, they gave her a car.

Maddy rarely talked about it.

Part of me figured that's why she had such bad taste in boys.

"Anyway, I had a dentist appointment this afternoon, so I'm sorry I didn't come by. But I'm cavity free and the dentist said that for as straight as my teeth are, I should never need braces."

"Nice," I said, looking at the TV. DJ had switched it from the news to a baseball game.

"Yeah. And I didn't finish there until almost four, so I just decided to come home instead."

"That's fine," I said. The pitcher had now thrown six pitches to the same batter.

This is why I dislike baseball.

Actually, sports in general. What's the point?

Answer — there is no point. It's a bunch of grown men in weird costumes accomplishing nothing.

I was never a big fan of those little-kid sports movies.

"Maddy," I said, before I forgot. "I think I'm going to stay home tomorrow, so could you bring my homework by after school?" Tomorrow was Friday. Maybe something drastic would happen over the weekend, and I could go back to school as just boring old Kate Carter. None of this Kate Escape business.

"You're staying home? This isn't because of what those mean old parents were talking about, is it? Because, gosh, Kate, they are just being ridiculous."

I thought about Officer DeWeise getting out of the hospital today and shook my head. "Maybe not so ridiculous, Maddy."

"Whatever. *I* think it's ridiculous."

"Anyway. Could you just gather up my homework for me?"

"I guess. I still think you should just come to school. But yeah, I'll get your homework. Need anything dropped off?"

I knew I had a big math test on Monday, but maybe the policemen could get my teacher to let me do a makeup. He hated giving makeups.

"I don't think so. Not right now, anyway."

"All right. I'll see you tomorrow afternoon then."

We hung up.

Friday morning dawned bright and sunny, and my eyes popped open at six forty-five out of sheer habit.

I was going to live to be one of those old people who couldn't sleep in if someone paid them.

I tried to roll over and go back to sleep, but my brain was already buzzing.

What if someone had identified the sketch I drew? What if that man was in prison right this very minute? What if Detective Masterson was making pancakes again for breakfast?

My stomach growled.

I sighed and gave up on going back to sleep. There was a stack of calculus textbooks from Dad next to the bed.

"I'm just worried that you'll be bored at home," he'd said last night at dinner.

Because calculus is usually the first thing I turn to when I get bored.

Mom had another option. "Why don't you get out that journal I gave you a long time ago and start writing down some of your thoughts?" she'd suggested.

That sounded about as fun as the calculus, considering my thought processes these days.

She'd given me the journal back in the eighth grade, and I'd written in it once.

Mom gave me this journal so I will grow up to be a healthy, active adult who cares about her psyche and her community.

Yay.

And that was all I'd written. I was pretty certain that journaling was not going to be my stress-relief method of choice.

I finally got out of bed at seven and went to take a shower. DJ was already up — his air mattress was already stowed out of the way. He and Detective Masterson were alternating sleeping on the mattress in the hallway during the night.

I had no idea how they still managed to carry on an intelligent conversation when they each only got about four hours of sleep every night. But I'd yet to hear them complain about being tired or even seen them yawn.

Policemen are a different breed of males.

I pulled on a pair of black track pants, white socks, and a white short-sleeve T-shirt after my shower. I ran the blow-dryer over my hair and decided to skip the straightening iron today.

After all, it was just me and the cops stuck at home today. And when someone has seen you talking in your sleep, you just don't have the same motivation to fix your hair as you did before that.

I did put on a little bit of makeup, though, to cover the dark circles under my eyes. Apparently, I still wasn't sleeping very well. I added some mascara and went to go see where everyone was.

Mom and Dad were sitting at the kitchen table, eating breakfast. DJ was leaning against the island counter reading the paper, and Detective Masterson wasn't around, which meant no pancakes.

Lolly was sleeping on the kitchen floor.

"Morning, Katie-Kin," Mom said, smiling at me. "How did you sleep?"

I shrugged, because that seemed like the safest answer.

"See, Claire? Even when she doesn't have school, Kate is up and ready to get to studying and increasing her knowledge. Isn't that right, Kate?" Dad said.

"Sure, Dad," I said, because again that seemed like the safest answer.

Since Mom had stopped buying me Crispix, my only choices for breakfast were Mini-Wheats or some weird granola stuff Mom liked.

I sighed. Mini-Wheats had a weird texture to me.

"There's toast too, honey," Mom said.

It sounded better than my other choices. I put two slices of bread in the toaster.

Detective Masterson walked in then, putting his cell phone in the pocket of his jeans. "Good morning, Kate," he said.

I nodded to his pocket. "Any leads on the sketch?"

He just gave me a short laugh. "Any? How about four hundred and thirty-nine? Apparently, everyone and their grandmother has seen this guy around town."

Mom looked up from her section of the paper. "Well, that's good then, isn't it?"

Detective Masterson shook his head. "Not really, ma'am. Whenever a well-publicized case like this is using a hotline, *everyone* wants in on the action. We can legitimately throw at least half of those tips into the garbage."

"Plus, since he was wearing sunglasses and a hooded sweatshirt, it makes it even more likely that we'll have a lot of tips that are just no good," DJ added.

My toast popped, and I spread a healthy layer of peanut butter all over it. I carried it over and sat down at the table with Mom and Dad.

"So the other half of the tips?" Dad asked.

Detective Masterson said, "We've got men checking those out today. A team from St. Louis came up and has been assisting Deputy Slalom in this investigation. Missourians are ready to relax again when they leave their houses."

Mom and Dad finished breakfast and then left about thirty minutes later. I was sitting on the floor in the living room petting Lolly when they headed out the door for work.

"Be careful," Dad said in his new way of saying good-bye.

"Journal," Mom said. "Try to write in your journal. And I'll call you later today."

They left.

I rubbed Lolly's silky ears, and she moaned like a cat. I reached over and pulled the remote off the coffee table. Surely something interesting was on TV at eight o'clock on a Friday morning.

I flipped through the channels for ten minutes. Or surely not. There were old sitcoms I'd never heard of playing reruns, Regis and Kelly were cracking not-so-funny jokes to an audience who was probably paid to laugh at them, a show where women found out they were pregnant in the delivery room, which just sounded ridiculous to me, and then a few true-crime shows.

I stopped on one of those, even though I knew I probably shouldn't be watching this stuff right now.

Detective Masterson came in before I really caught what was going on in the plot. So far, it was about an attorney who had a history of representing criminals who were most likely guilty and getting them off scot-free.

"What are you watching?" he asked, frowning at the TV.

I clicked the guide to see what the name of the episode was. He read it and immediately started shaking his head.

"Nope, nope. Sorry, Kate. You have enough nightmares as it is," he said, yanking the remote from my hand and turning the TV to Regis and Kelly.

Fabulous.

The day passed by very slowly. I watched mindless TV, painted my toenails, played tug-of-war with Lolly, and organized my bookshelf.

When I finished with my bookshelf, I looked at the clock, expecting it to be at least almost three and Maddy on her way here.

It was eleven. In the morning.

I sighed. I would never make it under house arrest. There was probably a good reason my parents never had to ground me. This was awful.

I went back out to the living room. Detective Masterson was reading something from a three-ring binder, and DJ was on the phone in the kitchen. Lolly sat with her head resting on the detective's feet. She would probably miss them when they didn't have to live here anymore.

"Bored out of your mind yet?" Detective Masterson grinned at me when I walked in and slumped on the couch.

"I don't understand why people skip school on purpose," I said. "There is absolutely nothing to do here."

"You could start on those calculus books," he said, grin widening.

"I haven't reached the suicidal stage of boredom yet." I looked around, thinking. I had no homework, there was nothing on TV, and I couldn't concentrate long enough to read anything.

"Any new leads?" I asked, hopefully.

Detective Masterson smiled at me. "Give them time, Kate. They'll find him."

I sighed.

He looked at me for a long minute and then closed his three-ring binder. "All right. What do you want to talk about?"

"What?" I asked.

"You're just going to sit there until Maddy shows up with your homework, aren't you?"

I shrugged. "I'll probably eat something in there too." I looked over at him. "This is what causes childhood obesity, huh?"

He grinned. "Witness protection?"

"House arrest."

"Considering the rise of childhood obesity and the few people every year who are put under protection, I'm thinking it's probably not the sole cause of it. Personally, I blame Xbox."

I'd never been a fan of video games. There were the kids at school who played them nonstop, and I'd always thought they were very strange people. They came in wearing their *Darth Vader could totally take Frodo* shirts, with their hair all straggly and their eyes all bloodshot.

Dad said that the effects of playing video games had to be similar to having a drinking binge the night before. He called it the "brain cell murderer."

"We aren't allowed to have an Xbox," I told the detective. "Dad thinks it ruins your brain cells, and Mom said it prohibits healthy family communication."

"You have smart parents," Detective Masterson said.

At noon, I turned the TV back on. *Miss Congeniality* was on and I watched the rest of it, snacking on deli meat and cheeses in the meantime.

Finally, the phone rang at two thirty. It was Maddy.

"So, Kate, about this whole bringing you your homework thing," she started.

I tried not to sigh too loudly, because that was Maddy's way of saying that she wasn't going to do it after all.

"Tyler asked if I wanted to go watch his football practice, and things are kind of on a slippery slope for us right now, so I really feel like I need to go do that if I'm going to make this work," she said.

"Didn't you guys just get back together yesterday?" I asked.

"No. Wednesday night."

"And things are already on a slippery slope?" I asked.

"We just have communication problems," she said.

Sometimes, Maddy and Tyler's problems seemed like they belonged more to a couple who had been married for ten years. I could just see them going to counseling for this.

"Well," I said. "Okay."

"Yeah, but don't you worry about getting your homework. I've already given it to someone else, and they're coming by."

It was probably Allison Northing, and I'd have to listen to her chatter mindlessly for an hour before she'd leave and let me get to studying.

Even though mindless chatter was totally welcome at this point in my house. Detective Masterson was back to reading from his three-ring binder, and DJ was again on the phone.

"Okay," I said. "Have fun at the practice."

"Thanks, Kate! Have a fun day at home! You are so lucky you got to stay home all day, by the way."

"Not really," I said. "Bye."

Detective Masterson looked over at me when I hung up. "No homework?"

"She sent it with Allison Northing. Remember the girl who sat next to me in art class?"

He didn't do a very good job at hiding his wince.

"Yeah. Just be prepared," I said, sounding an awfully lot like Scar in *The Lion King*.

Fifteen minutes later, my doorbell rang. DJ answered it, since I was not allowed to answer the door alone.

I steeled myself, waiting for Allison's loud voice.

I didn't hear anything. A second later, DJ walked into the living room followed by Justin Walters.

I was a little bit shocked. Or a lot bit.

"Hi, Allison," Detective Masterson greeted him, grinning. "You look different outside of school."

Justin smiled confusedly at the detective. "I'm Justin Walters. I have Kate's homework," he said, like he was being interrogated.

"Sure you do," Detective Masterson said, still grinning. "I'll just go get something to drink. DJ, you want something?"

DJ was standing behind Justin and looking at me. "What? Oh yeah. That sounds great."

They both left, leaving me and Silent Justin standing in the living room.

Lolly wagged over to Justin, and he petted her ears. "Pretty dog," he said, though I wasn't sure if it was directed to me or Lolly.

"Thanks for bringing my homework," I said after a minute. First, Justin doesn't talk to me for three straight years — well, almost — and now he's bringing me my homework.

It was a little awkward, to say the least.

"Sure, no problem," he said, handing me a stack of papers.

"Miss Yeager's homework is to pick one of the careers we talked about and draw something for that career. She said you didn't have to do it, though."

I frowned. "How come?" Suddenly I'm not only not welcome at school but I can't even do the homework?

I felt like a homebound invalid. Next thing we knew, someone was going to be calling that traveling meal service to come feed me.

Justin must have seen the anger, because he immediately stopped petting Lolly and put both hands up. "Just because she said that you had already done it," he said quickly, in a soothing voice. "She said you'd already done it at least twice, which was all the rest of us were required to do."

So Miss Yeager had recognized my work on TV again.

I sighed. "If it's an assignment, then I'm going to do it too."

"Fine by me," Justin said.

"What are you going to do?"

He shrugged. "I don't know. I kind of like restaurant and commercial art. Honestly, it's just a hobby."

This was the most he'd ever talked to me, so I tried to keep the conversation going. "What do you want to do then?"

Another shrug. "I'm good at math. I've thought about engineering."

I just looked at him.

What is with me and this apparent magnetic force I have toward engineers? My dad. My brother. Now Justin.

Justin is the only one of those three, though, who appreciates art. My dad and Mike think art is a waste of time and a ridiculous use of pencil lead.

"Oh?" I said, because I couldn't think of anything else to say.

"Yeah. And with the art background, I'm kind of interested in something along the lines of architectural engineering."

"So you want to design buildings?"

He shrugged. Yet again. "I don't know. Maybe. It's a thought, anyway. I still have two years to decide."

"Well. A year and a half."

"Yeah." He finished scratching behind Lolly's ear and looked at me. "So, what do you want to do?" Then he grinned. "That might be kind of an obvious answer, huh?"

My turn to shrug. "I don't know." I sat down on the couch. "Do you think that if you are good at something that's a sign you should do it?"

He thought about it for a minute and sat on the recliner. Lolly scrambled over to lay her head in his lap.

"Not necessarily," he said. "Like, my sister is good at cooking but she's a finance major at Missouri State."

"You have a sister?"

He nodded. "And a younger brother. He's nine."

So much I didn't know about this guy. It was amazing that we'd been sitting next to each other in classes for the entire last year.

I looked over at him. "How come you don't talk like this at school?"

"I don't know. Allison talks enough for the entire class. And I like to just concentrate at school." He leaned back in the recliner. "So does that mean you don't really want to be a forensic sketch artist?" he asked, going back to my earlier question.

I sighed as I thought about it. On the one hand, I loved the art aspect of it. Faces had always intrigued me and I'd always loved to draw them. And the idea that I was helping people by doing it. That was cool.

On the other hand, I didn't like this part of the job. The staying in hiding, getting shot at, worrying about my friends and family and the people protecting me part of it.

Surely not *all* sketching jobs for the police department were this dangerous though. I mean, look at Larry, whoever he was. He was apparently safe. Unemployed, but safe.

Poor Larry.

I realized Justin was watching me then and I shook my head. "I like parts of it. I don't like other parts of it."

"Sounds like any job then," Justin said. "My dad is an attorney. He said that he really likes the helping people and the money parts of it, but he hates the actual legal process."

"Why did he become an attorney then?"

Justin grinned suddenly. "Because my mom was in school to be a legal assistant, and Dad thought she was cute."

"That's funny," I said, smiling.

"Yeah. So did you draw the picture of the guy they think shot at you at the parade?" he asked.

I nodded.

"It was a good picture."

"Thanks."

"Think you'll come back to church on Sunday?"

I hadn't even thought about it. It was more Mom's thing than mine anyway. "I don't know," I said. "Maybe. We'll see what happens by the time Sunday gets here."

He smiled. "It's only two days away."

"A lot can happen in two days."

"If you come, you should come to the second service. It's more laid back."

I thought about Sister Elizabeth Parker and her boisterously loud amens. For being such a tiny woman, she could sure get loud.

"Do people say amen as much?" I asked.

He shook his head. "Hardly ever. Why? Do people say it a lot in the first service? I haven't been to first service in years."

"Oh yeah," I said, nodding. "A ton. Like Sister Elizabeth Parker? She gets nice and loud. I jumped every time Sister said it."

He grinned widely. "You know, Kate, you don't have to call them 'sister' and 'brother' unless you just want to," he said.

"What?" I asked.

"Sister Elizabeth Parker? Her name isn't sister."

I just looked at him. "Then why did she introduce herself as Sister?"

"Because sometimes people in the church say that as a way of saying that we're all part of the body of Christ." He was still grin-ning. "Her name is just Elizabeth Parker."

Christians were very weird.

And I felt pretty dumb. "Well," I said, fumbling around for some shred of pride left. "Since you know everything, where is Zion and why are we marching there?"

He just laughed.

Chapter Fifteen

SATURDAY AT NOON, DEPUTY SLALOM CALLED DETECTIVE Masterson. I could hear the deputy's deep voice over the phone even though Detective Masterson was sitting on the other end of the couch from me. We'd been playing a game of Phase 10.

Dad was killing us all.

I think it was starting to bug DJ. I never noticed he was competitive until right then.

"One second," Detective Masterson whispered to all of us and stood and walked into the kitchen.

It was Mom's turn, and she was busy staring at the top card on the discard pile.

"Pause," DJ said, rolling his shoulders and laying on his back on the floor. We were all gathered around the coffee table. Mom and DJ were sitting on the floor, Dad had the recliner, and the detective and I had the sofa.

Mom laid her cards face down and then started doing a couple of back stretches.

"Do you want to sit here?" I asked her for the thirtieth time that day.

She shook her head. "I sit on a couch all week long, Kate. I like the floor."

Mom's office had two couches in it. One for her and one for her patient. Sometimes I think she sat at her desk, but the majority of the time she was on the couch.

I nodded and everyone got quiet. I think we were all trying to overhear Detective Masterson's conversation in the kitchen, but he was talking too quietly for us to hear.

Dad was looking at the score sheet. He had his glasses on, which I thought made him look at least fifteen years older.

"So, I'm on phase six, Kent is on phase five, and you three are all still on phase four," he said.

I could see DJ stiffening on the floor. "I hate this game," he mumbled.

"What was that, DJ?" I asked.

He sat up. "Nothing." Then she shot a look of challenge at my dad. "It can all change in one hand, Dale. Just one hand."

"Heh. We'll see," Dad said.

My dad can be quite the competitive person as well.

Detective Masterson came back in the room then, sliding his cell phone back into the pocket of his jeans. All of us immediately quit talking and looked up at him.

"Kate, you've got a press conference at three," he said, squinting at the clock over the fireplace.

"Press conference?" I asked.

"What?" Mom said.

"I thought you guys said that wasn't a good idea." Dad frowned.

"Also, we've had three separate leads all tell us that they saw a man who fit the description of the one you drew at a grocery store in Ballwin. We've got a team headed over there right now." He sat on the couch and picked up his cards.

Ballwin is closer to St. Louis than South Woodhaven Falls. It's almost straight to the west of the city, and we're more to the northwest.

"Is that what I'm supposed to talk about then?" I asked.

"What?" he said.

"The lead. The grocery store?"

"Oh," Detective Masterson said, shaking his head. "No, no. You just need to talk about drawing. Don't mention anything about the lead. We don't want this guy to leave Ballwin if he hasn't already."

A press conference.

I tried to hide the groan. I thought I'd gotten out of giving a press conference.

"So, we'll leave here around two or two fifteen to give you time to get ready, okay?" Detective Masterson said. "You'll be giving it at the station, so don't worry about safety." He said that mostly to my dad.

"Great! Let's play," DJ said, picking up his cards.

"So I'm just supposed to talk about drawing?" I asked.

Detective Masterson nodded, and DJ laid his cards face down again. "Just talk about your techniques, your excitement over John X being caught, and how you're hoping this new drawing will bring enough notice to find his accomplice," he said.

He made it sound very easy.

"Ready?" DJ asked as soon as the detective stopped talking, grabbing his cards again. "Ready to play?"

"What are you, six?" I asked him, rolling my eyes.

He shrugged. "I have to beat your dad, Kate."

"Just so you know, Dad has not lost at Phase 10 since he had the Great Stomach Flu of 2003, and even then, he didn't actually *lose*, he quit early because he couldn't stop throwing up."

DJ made a face. "Is that true, sir?"

Dad nodded. "Man, that was a miserable night. I rarely get sick, but that night I thought it was the end of the line for me." He looked at Mom. "Remember that night, Claire?"

She sighed. "How could I forget? You made me pull out the will and go over it before you went to sleep." She was rolling her eyes now too. "All men are hypochondriacs."

DJ said, "I meant about the Phase 10 record, not the stomach flu."

"Oh," Dad said. "Yes, it's true."

He straightened. "Well, it ends today."

Dad just shook his head. "Words I've heard before. Never seen the fruit of it, though."

Detective Masterson looked over at me. "So, you're good for today?"

"Do I have a choice?" I asked.

"Not really."

I shrugged. "Then does it matter?"

He looked at his cards. "I guess not. Just ask me if you need help preparing something. Mostly it will just be a chance for people like Ted Deffle to finally ask you some questions."

"Maybe he'll stop sending flowers then," Mom said. "I love flowers, I really do. But when it takes me thirty minutes just to water all of them and when the air in my house is starting to get a yellowish pollen hue to it, I start to think otherwise."

It would be nice. We had three more bouquets today. One was from KCL and the other two were from people in Springfield, Missouri.

We finished playing the game — Dad won again much to DJ's distress — and I went to go find something to wear to the press conference.

What in the world are you supposed to wear to press conferences? The only ones I've ever seen involved people confessing that yes, they did cheat on their wives just like the whole country knew they had. They always wore a collared polo shirt and sunglasses.

I would assume the attire would be different for today's occasion.

Mom knocked on the open door, while I stood and stared at my closet.

"Need some help?" she asked, coming in.

"Skirt or pants? Short sleeve or long sleeve?" I tugged on a couple of clothes but didn't pull them out of the closet.

Mom let out a long sigh. "Well," she said, coming next to me to join in staring at my closet. "I'm always a fan of longer sleeves on

TV. I think it makes your face more of the focus instead of people staring at your arms."

I found a couple of three-quarter-length shirts and pulled them out. It was too warm to wear long sleeves.

"And I would just wear jeans. You're sixteen, and you'll probably be sitting down," Mom said, shrugging. "You might as well be comfortable."

She had a point. So I picked out a cranberry-colored, three-quarter-length shirt and my favorite pair of jeans. Mom told me to pick the cranberry top because, apparently, I was a person who looked better in winter colors.

Until then, I had no idea that cranberry was in any way associated with winter other than being a traditional side dish for Christmas dinner.

For once, my hair actually straightened correctly, and I practiced smiling without squinting as I put on my makeup.

"Time to go, Kate," Detective Masterson said as I came out of my room.

I nodded. We all piled into the Tahoe, and DJ drove us to the police station.

The good old familiar police station.

Tons of news vans were there. South Woodhaven Falls only has one news crew, KCL, so I asked DJ as we pulled to a stop in front of the building where all the other vans had driven from for this conference.

"All over," he said, shrugging. "Like that one? WGDB? I think they are one of the main ones in Saint Louis."

A few news people and their cameras were gathered out front of the building, but DJ and Detective Masterson hustled me in so I didn't even hear their barrage of questions.

Plenty of time for that soon.

The station had two conference rooms. One was the conference room that I'd sketched the parade shooter in and where I'd met with Deputy Slalom. The other I'd never been in. It was much larger and had enough room for about fifty people to sit comfortably. There was a long table at the front of the room on some risers.

"I have to sit there by myself?" I whispered to DJ.

He shook his head. "Kent's going up there with you. And so is the boss."

That made me feel a little better. I was also glad I hadn't worn a skirt. That would have put the edge of my hem on eye level with the cameras.

A lady stepped up on the risers and attached a couple of microphones onto the table.

People were milling around everywhere. Mostly well-made-up people wearing suits with big, coiffed hair and earpieces. Cameras blocked every possible walkway.

Deputy Slalom walked in then and clapped his hands. "All right, let's do this," he said, climbing up on the riser. He was dressed nicely today. Slacks, a button-down collared shirt, and a sport coat.

I looked like a little kid they'd dragged out of school next to him.

Which was sort of the truth.

Detective Masterson was wearing his uniform, which had become kind of a rare sight for me. He helped me climb onto the tall riser, and I sat down in the middle chair.

I felt like a little person. Deputy Slalom is probably an inch or two over six feet tall, and he's shaped like a big barrel. Detective Masterson isn't a big man, but he is tall. He really does look a lot like a tougher Orlando Bloom.

And then there was all five feet one of me. In front of a table that sat a few inches higher than a normal table, and I had to reach a microphone on top of that.

The people with the news crews were slowly arranging themselves on the chairs below. The cameras were mostly in the back and along the sides of the room.

I felt like I needed to make an apology to my significant other.

Thanks to my No Dating High School Boys rule, though, I wouldn't have to deal with that.

"All right, all right," Deputy Slalom said gruffly, pulling his microphone closer. "Everyone take a seat, we're going to make this short and sweet."

I wondered if he realized he rhymed.

I pulled the microphone closer to me as well, and it squealed super loud in protest. Everyone in the room groaned and covered their ears.

"Sorry," I muttered.

Detective Masterson grinned at me. "Ladies and gentlemen, thank you for coming today on such short notice, but you can understand why, considering the security breach at the parade last week. You'll have fifteen minutes to talk to Kate Carter, so please make your questions brief. Kate, go ahead."

Go ahead and what? I just smiled — being careful to avoid squinting — and looked around. "Um. Any questions?" I asked.

All of the reporters started shouting right then, so loud that I couldn't make out one question from another.

Deputy Slalom rolled his eyes. "One at a time!" he yelled darkly into the microphone. Then he pointed. "You. Talk."

It was Ted Deffle from KCL. I half wondered then if he'd been sending flowers to the police station as well, and that's why he got picked first.

"Kate, Ted Deffle from KCL," he said, standing and flashing his teeth that were so white they probably caused traffic accidents.

"Hi, Ted," I said.

"Let's start with John X. How did you manage to draw such a picture-perfect image? And were you the artist who created the portrait of the proposed shooter at the parade?"

I looked briefly at Detective Masterson, who just smiled encouragingly at me. "Well," I said, "I heard a description of what John X looked like, and I just drew what I saw." Simple enough answer. "And yeah, I drew the shooter at the parade."

"Kate! KATE!"

"Enough!" Deputy Slalom yelled again. He pointed. "You. Go."

Another man, this one with hair that looked like he'd emptied a can of shine serum into it.

Ew.

"Hi, Kate, Ralph Robins from Springfield. I think we're all wondering the same thing," he said. "You're sixteen, you're a junior in high school, and you're not even old enough to vote. How is it that you are the one who is now drawing all these criminals? Might I say, very *dangerous* criminals?"

He was looking more at Deputy Slalom and Detective Masterson than he was at me, but the question was still addressed to me, so I cleared my throat.

"Well, um, I don't think you can ever be too young to assist your country when it's in need," I said, trying not to flinch. Now I sounded like a miniature politician. Cue the national anthem and the big flag dropping behind me.

Detective Masterson leaned forward then. "Every measure has been taken to ensure Kate and her family's safety and health during this time. We have also been very aware of child labor laws and are actively guarding Kate's delicate psyche."

I glanced over at my mom, who was nodding like Sister Elizabeth Parker during the preacher's sermon last Sunday. I was almost waiting for a loud "amen!"

Deputy Slalom pointed out a brunette lady this time whose hair was teased so high, I had trouble seeing any cameras behind her.

"Cindy Treller from St. Louis. Kate, why did you lean forward at the parade?"

Oh, the question of the week.

I still got a tight, tingly feeling in my gut when I thought about it. Sort of like when you find out that you're going to have to get shots at your doctor's visit and it was never just a checkup.

I looked around for a minute, trying to figure out what I was going to say. "I don't know," I said, honestly. "I had put my sunglasses in my purse on the backseat, and we were starting to get to the part of the parade that was in the sun. So, I was trying to pull my sunglasses out." I took a deep breath. "Why it was at that particular moment, I don't know."

Detective Masterson and Justin would say that God was watching out for me.

I thought that God, if there really was a God, had better things to do than worry about what a five-foot-nothing average student was doing.

On and on the questions came.

"Have you always liked art?" one man with something of an afro asked.

"I assume that a career as a criminal sketch artist is in your future?" a lady wearing a suit that looked like it was from the eighties said.

"Anything you'd care to say to John X?"

The last question was from a man in the back. He was tall, blond, and had the prettiest chocolate-brown eyes I'd ever seen. He'd introduced himself as Rick Litchfield from a southern St. Louis station.

If I lived in St. Louis, I would definitely be watching his news station.

I wasn't a huge fan of his questioning skills though.

I thought about it, looking at the big green x in the EXIT sign hanging over the conference room's closed doors.

If I had anything to say to John X ...

I would want to know why. Why did he kill those four innocent women? They hadn't done anything to him, he didn't know them from anywhere. They were just moms, wives, girlfriends minding their own business, going about their own day. Not causing any harm to anyone.

I would want to know if he was sorry. Judging from the one picture I'd seen of him in prison, I would guess no, but it never hurt to ask.

I would want to know how many people he had working for him. He had at least one friend who liked to wear a hooded sweatshirt. How many more?

I leaned forward to the microphone. "I'd say enjoy that prison pot roast."

The reporters all started laughing. Rick Litchfield in the back smiled.

"Good answer," he said.

"That does it for today," Deputy Slalom said gruffly. "Thank you for coming to the press conference, enjoy your day."

Both he and Detective Masterson stood, and I followed suit. We stepped off the risers and they escorted me, Mom, and Dad into Deputy Slalom's office.

"Great job, honey," Mom said, giving me a hug. "You looked beautiful up there."

"Did you really have to end with a threat to John X?" Dad asked, face tight. "Come on, Kate."

I shrugged. "It wasn't a threat." I looked at Detective Masterson. "Did it sound like a threat?"

He looked at me and my dad and chose his words carefully. "It was a, uh, tease," he said. "But you managed to end on a light note and for that, I'm grateful. Coffee, anyone? Tea? Coke?"

"Coke," I said. Deputy Slalom was nodding to the chairs in front of his desk, so I sat.

"Nothing, thanks," Dad said, sitting down next to me. Mom asked for a bottle of water and then sat on the other side of me.

Detective Masterson went to go get the drinks, and Deputy Slalom sat behind his desk, knitted his fingers together, and laid his fists on the desk.

"So, we'll just hang out in here for a bit, just so they all leave." He looked out his window where several of the news people were now giving reports in the parking lot. He sighed. "Might be awhile."

Detective Masterson came back with my Coke, a bottle of water for Mom, and two Snapple Peach Teas. He handed one to the deputy and kept the other for himself.

"Anyway, good job, Kate. I thought you did very well handling yourself," Deputy Slalom said in his gruff voice after a long swig of peach tea.

"Thanks."

"Professional and short answers. I like that."

I nodded. "Did anything turn up at that grocery store in Ballwin?" I asked.

He took another long sip of his tea. "Not yet, Kate. Give it time. We've got a team down there, but phone tips can take weeks, if not months, to turn up anything."

"You guys got John X awfully quick," I said.

"That was completely a matter of being at the right place and at the right time with the right photograph," he said. "I heard you aren't going to school anymore." He looked at Dad as he said it.

"Yes, sir. And it's completely my decision," I said, taking the blame away from my dad. "The parents of the other kids at school were starting to keep their kids home so they wouldn't have to worry about them standing in the same hallway as me and getting shot."

Deputy Slalom rolled his eyes. "It's those panicky people that make my job so much harder than it really is," he said. "The last thing this guy or John X wants is another murder other than yours to chalk up to his name. He's already facing the death penalty. Committing a crime against a minor isn't going to help his case."

I popped the top on my Coke. "Still, that's the way it is at South Woodhaven Falls High."

"Okay. Well, hopefully, something will turn up on this shooter in Ballwin. In the meantime, keep up with your studies. And, Kate," he said, his voice getting softer, "did you get a chance to consider my offer from last time?"

I shook my head in mid-swallow. "No, sir. Not yet."

"No worries," he said. "Take your time."

Mom and Dad were looking at me curiously, but I did my best to ignore them and finish my Coke.

There would be plenty of time for questions later.

Chapter Sixteen

SUNDAY MORNING AND MOM DECIDED WE WERE ALL GOING to church again. "I don't know what's going on here right now, but I know that we can't handle this by ourselves," she said last night at dinner. "Now, DJ and Kent will be along with us to watch out for Kate's safety, so we have no excuses," she said, cutting off my dad before he even got a word out of his open mouth.

I was pretty sure that Dad wasn't too excited about it.

But we all piled into the Tahoe at ten o'clock on Sunday morning. I was wearing a pair of jeans and a nicer top. Detective Masterson had dressed up in khakis and a button-down. Mom was wearing one of her business suits minus the jacket.

The first service was just leaving at South Woodhaven Falls First Baptist Church when we got there. I saw Sister Elizabeth Parker talking animatedly with the man who stood on the stage asking for amens last week.

"Kate!" someone yelled.

I looked around and Justin Walters was waving at me, leaving his group of friends to come say hi.

"I'm glad you came," he said, smiling. "You're just getting here, right?"

I nodded, noticing Detective Masterson not-so-subtly grin at DJ. "Yes, we just got here," I said loudly, moving so the two cops weren't behind me. Hopefully, Justin didn't notice them.

He grinned wider. "Great! You guys can sit with my family. Come on in." He waved to his group of friends and led us into the big meeting room.

It looked a lot different from last week. The organ was still on the stage, but it was buried behind a set of drums. Three guitars, a bass, lots of microphones, and a few skinny, punked-out guys were up there. The guys were milling around, adjusting their girl pants and swiping their longish hair out of their eyes.

I glanced over at Dad, who was already shaking his head. I don't think Dad liked the hymns last week, but he really hates men in women's clothing or hairstyles. Dad believes that all guys should have buzz cuts and wear pants that fit relaxed in the rear and legs.

Justin had a buzz cut. And was wearing simple, straight-cut jeans.

"Guys, this is my mom and dad," he said, pointing to one pew where a blonde woman and a gray-haired man sat. "Lucinda and Jason," he said.

My parents introduced themselves, and I shook their hands as well. We introduced DJ and the detective as old family friends.

Lucinda clasped my hand tightly. "How are you, dear? We've been praying so hard for you!"

"Uh, good. Thanks." Her hand was squeezing my first and fourth knuckles together. It kind of hurt.

"Yes, we have!" Justin's dad boomed. "And Dale, if you need anything, you just holler, okay?" He clapped my dad's shoulder.

Dad just nodded.

Someone plucked a couple of strings on a guitar, and the lights immediately dimmed everywhere except for the stage. We all filed into the pew, except for DJ, who was going to stand in the back. He whispered some lame excuse about having a bad back to Lucinda when she protested that there was plenty of room in the pew.

I knew he was back there to keep an eye on things. I sat between Dad and Detective Masterson and looked up at the stage.

"Hi," one of the girly looking guys said. "My name is Shaun, and welcome to SWF First Baptist. Let's worship, shall we?"

He strummed down his electric guitar, and the drummer and other two guitarists and bass player picked up the beat.

Shaun started to sing and the words suddenly appeared behind him on a big screen that I hadn't noticed last week.

The weird, flamboyant monk outfits were nowhere to be seen. Everyone around us immediately stood and started singing, raising their hands and moving to the beat of the music.

I felt like I was at a concert. Only, a weird, sing-along concert.

It sounded like the detective knew all the words. I could hear Mom trying to sing along as well. Dad just stood and stared at the stage.

I tried to sing. There was no mention of Zion or dost or thou or any of those weird words that I wasn't sure what they meant.

"We are hungry, we are hungry," the lead guy sang. He really had a great voice. And while the song was actually making me hungry, I did enjoy listening to it.

I peeked around Dad and Mom and saw Justin singing with his eyes closed and his right hand lifted about waist high.

I didn't get the raising hands thing. It was like half the people here were calling that it was their turn to sing next or saying they had a question.

I had a question. If we were so hungry, why were they only serving the tiniest fragments of crackers and the smallest glasses of grape juice I'd ever seen to wash it down with? It was like what I imagined you gave an infant for their first meal.

The same man who talked last Sunday got back on the stage. Only now he wasn't wearing a suit coat or a tie or even nice pants. He'd pulled the tail of his button-down shirt out and had changed into straight-cut jeans.

"Thanks, Shaun," he said into his wireless lapel microphone. No more standing behind a lectern, he just carried a worn Bible and carried a stool over to the middle of the stage.

"Good morning," he said warmly, sitting on the stool and opening his Bible. He taught for about thirty minutes, and he didn't once say the word "amen" except at the end of a prayer.

No one said it in the audience either. And after he finished teaching, the band came back up and did one more chorus from one of the songs they'd sung earlier.

Afterward, the people around me exploded out of their seats.

"Hi!" one very exuberant boy about the age of ten or so said, popping up behind me. "You're Kate Carter!"

I nodded. "What's your name?"

"James," he said, grinning, two dimples appearing on both of his cheeks.

Justin stood and leaned around Mom and Dad. "This is my little brother."

"Oh," I said. "Well, nice to meet you, James."

A bunch of people came over then to talk to the new family, I guess, but I noticed that Detective Masterson was looking more and more anxious about the growing crowd.

"Wow, Kate Carter!" one high school–aged boy said, coming over. "I'm Sam Lawry, and can I say that you are one of the bravest girls I've ever heard of?" He stuck out his hand to me. "I've always hoped we'd meet at school, but the grade difference probably prevents it."

I squinted at him. *Sam Lawry* was ringing bells and I wasn't sure why. "Have we met already?" I asked, and even though it sounded like a horrendous pickup line, I really thought we'd already met.

"I play on the football team," he said, grinning one of those "I'm important" smiles at me. "Defensive end."

He could have told me the name of the part of the car that makes it go forward for all I understood about his last sentence. "Cool," I said like I knew what he meant.

"We should get together and talk or something," he said.

Right then, three squealing girls ran over.

"WE SAW YOU ON TV!" they screamed.

"Oh my gosh, that was *so* cool," another guy chimed in.

Soon, it was a loud madhouse. I couldn't see my parents anymore. Somehow, I'd gotten sucked into this circle of kids who were all going crazy.

Detective Masterson reached into the mob, grabbed my forearm, and hustled me toward the door. "No more teenage hormones," he mumbled as he yanked me outside.

DJ was also looking concerned as he hurried over to help get Mom and Dad, and the two cops rushed us to the Tahoe.

"Okay," Detective Masterson sighed when we were all in the car. "Kate, no offense to your social life, but I liked it better when no one wanted to talk to you."

Mom frowned her disapproval of his comment but refrained from making one herself.

Dad was shaking his head. "Did you see the pants on that singer guy?"

I had to smile.

We got home and piled out of the Tahoe. The day was beautiful. I sniffed. Something smelled really good. One of our neighbors must be barbecuing.

I walked to the front door and stopped.

Instead of the usual assortment of flowers, there was a pan covered in aluminum foil sitting right in front of the door.

Detective Masterson joined me, saw the pan, and immediately moved into police mode. He called for DJ to come help him and together they slowly approached the pan. One of them reached down and pulled a white card off the top of it.

In the process, they nudged the foil, and the savory scent of roasting beef was even stronger.

I froze.

"What is it?" Mom asked, slinging her purse over her shoulder. She squinted at the foil-covered meat and nodded. "See? People should always send food instead of flowers. I wish this idea had caught on a long time ago."

I stayed rooted where I was on the porch. Detective Masterson's chin was set so hard, I worried about his back molars.

DJ exchanged a look first with the detective and then with me.

"What is it?" Dad asked, echoing Mom behind me.

It was a pot roast.

Barely ten minutes passed by before our yard was swimming with cops. Uniforms were everywhere — in the house, in the bushes, combing the neighbors' yard.

The fabulous-smelling pot roast had gotten shipped off to the police station for testing, but not before I'd seen the note.

I'm nothing if not generous, Kate.

It wasn't signed, but we all knew who it was from. He had nice handwriting, that friend of John X's.

I was watching out the front window. A forensics team was scouring the front yard for footprints, hair, anything that might lead them to the shooter from the parade.

DJ came back inside then, pulling a pair of aviator sunglasses off his face. He looked over at me. "You doing okay, Kate?"

I nodded. I was kneeling on the couch, holding the curtain back with one hand, my chin balanced on the back of my other hand, which was on the back of the couch.

I watched as two policemen bagged just about everything in our front yard except for Mom's frog garden decoration that sat in the front flower pot. But sod, dirt, leaves — you name it, and it got stuck in a bag with a label on it.

"Look at it this way, Kate. It was a pot roast. It wasn't a gun, it wasn't someone waiting for us when we got home. It was just a harmless pot roast."

Harmless to everyone except the cow, I guess.

I nodded again, though, because I knew that was what DJ wanted me to do. "Okay," I said.

He gave me a sad smile and went into the kitchen, where Detective Masterson and a few other cops were having a powwow around our kitchen table.

Mom and Dad were sitting on the other couch. Dad hadn't said anything else about the pot roast comment I'd made, but I knew he was thinking it.

I felt bad. If I'd just brushed off the reporter's question, our house wouldn't have become the newest branch of the South Woodhaven Falls police department.

I should've just said that I didn't have anything to say to John X.

I let the drape fall back down and turned to look at Mom and Dad. They were watching the news. All media vans had been blocked at the top of the street, so they were reporting from the corner.

"And I'm getting another report, hang on a second," Candace Olstrom, the peppy, blonde reporter, squealed to the camera. She turned to a guy I didn't recognize who wasn't from the police department, because he wasn't in uniform, and talked to him quietly for a minute. Then she turned back to the camera.

"Well, it seems that authorities are still busy trying to find out who left a mysterious package on heroine Kate Carter's doorstep earlier this afternoon."

Shocking report. I stood and went to my room.

I sat down at my desk and tried to think about my homework. It was Sunday, after all. Justin was going to drop by tomorrow morning on his way to school to pick up my completed assignments.

Or at least he was before this fiasco.

I'd finished my math and science homework. I had a take-home quiz in English, but that wouldn't take me more than about half an hour to do.

I pulled over my sketchpad. Miss Yeager had wanted us to draw something that was an example of what we wanted to do in an art-centered career.

I closed my eyes for a minute.

John X's face had been replaced in my brain by the parade shooter. I'd already drawn him though.

I started just sketching whatever came to mind.

I could still smell the remnants of pot roast in the house. My stomach began growling, and I remembered that I'd never eaten lunch.

The sketch started to have a face.

Medium-spaced brown eyes framed by thick, whiteish-blond eyelashes. Freckles stood out along the cheekbones. A straight, red-haired buzz cut with a nice hairline.

I worked on it for about an hour and then went into the kitchen, hoping the police had found a new meeting spot.

But they were all still there. Maps were spread on the table and people were talking softly, using words like "perpetrator."

I tried my best to sneak in so I could just quickly make a sand-wich and leave. I had the bread out of the pantry when Detective Masterson looked over and saw me.

"Kate," he said, and everyone stopped talking and looked over at me.

Now I felt like I was stealing bread from my own house. "I was just making a sandwich," I said quickly.

He smiled then. "You aren't in trouble. Are you okay?" He stood from the table and came over, leaning against the counter while I grabbed a package of deli turkey meat, mustard, swiss cheese, and lettuce from the fridge.

The other people around the table started talking again.

I shrugged. "I'm fine," I said, pulling my standard facing-the-doctor answer out for him. "Sorry to interrupt. I'm just getting lunch."

He looked at the clock on the oven and sighed. "It's late for lunch. I'm so sorry about all this, Kate."

Another shrug. "I'm the one who had to make the pot roast reference at the press conference."

"If it's any consolation, it was a really funny reference," he said, trying to lighten the mood.

I spread a thin layer of mustard on the bread and stacked on the turkey, lettuce, and cheese. "I thought so too."

"We will find him, you know," he said in a quiet voice. "And everything will go back to normal for you."

Funny how it had only been two weeks and I could barely remember what normal looked like for me.

Justin rang my doorbell at seven o'clock the next morning. I hadn't slept more than about two hours Sunday night thanks to more nightmares, so I was up, showered, and reading *The Grapes of Wrath*, since we had to have it finished by the end of the school year.

Which was in almost six months. Better to get a head start on it now.

I was so bored I was scaring myself.

DJ opened the door and escorted Justin into the family room. "Morning, Kate," Justin said, looking all awake and refreshed after what could only have been a great night's sleep.

He looked around my living room. I was slumped on the sofa, eyes bleary. DJ had black circles so thick under his eyes that he looked like he could have been playing on a football team. Detective Masterson was rubbing a three-day-old beard, and Mom and Dad were silently eating breakfast, staring at the table.

"Lively bunch today," Justin said to me.

I rubbed my eyes. "It was a long day yesterday."

He nodded. "I heard about that. Someone left a package on your doorstep? What was it? Was it a bomb or something?"

"No. It was a pot roast."

He was quiet for a minute, staring at me. Finally he cleared his throat. "Maybe I'm missing something, but I actually like pot roast, and I'm not sure why someone leaving one of those would cause so much sleepiness today." His eyes widened. "Unless the pot roast was drugged or something."

I think that Justin has watched too many crime shows on TV. Either that or read too many Hardy Boys books as a kid.

"We didn't eat it," I said. "I made a comment about how I hope John X is enjoying his prison pot roast at the press conference, and then one showed up on my doorstep."

DJ started clearing his throat, and I guessed I'd talked too much. "But anyway," I said offhandedly, like it was no big deal and we were just all completely zombied-out for no reason at all. I grabbed my stack of papers for him. "Here's my homework. Thanks again for doing this, Justin."

He tucked the papers into his backpack. "Sure, no problem. You positive you don't want to come to school today? I came here a few minutes early to try and talk you into it."

I shook my head. "Nope. I'm putting myself under house arrest until this guy is caught and happily eating his share of the prison pot roast."

Justin quirked his head. "Do they even serve pot roast in prison? I mean, I'm no expert, but I've seen a few of those documentary things they show on TV about life in the slammer, and I've never seen anyone eating a pot roast." He shrugged. "But then again, I don't think I've ever really seen anyone eating. I think that show likes to only show the fight scenes."

Must have been the same documentary I'd watched before. We both just looked over at Detective Masterson, who was skimming the paper through red-rimmed, sleep-deprived eyes.

He looked up at us after a few seconds. "What?" he asked.

"Do they serve pot roast in prison?" I asked. I'd asked DJ before and he hadn't been sure.

Detective Masterson shrugged. "You'd need to contact a warden with that question. But I can tell you that one of the times I was there they were serving meat loaf." He rolled a shoulder. "I guess that's almost like pot roast."

Except it's much grosser.

My mother hated meat loaf with a passion. I could only think of one time that we'd had meat loaf in this house, and it was when my grandfather died and some people from my dad's work brought dinner for us.

Mom said it was like the bologna of dinner meats. She said that someone out there must have not wanted to go grocery shopping that day so she just threw everything she had into a bowl, mixed it all together, and baked it, and unfortunately invented meat loaf.

Mom could barely even stand to say the words. She called it "that horrendous meat product."

My dad, on the other hand, loved meat loaf. He said that my grandmother used to make it all the time for them for dinner when he was growing up. "It's an amazing meal," he told me one time after one of Mom's tirades on it. "Cheesy, melty, juicy ..." Then he'd just sighed and poked at the plain chicken breast on his plate.

Justin shrugged. "Well, anyway. I know there aren't kitchens in the jail cells, though, so how did John X get the pot roast over to you?"

At the conclusion of yesterday's cop invasion, they'd decided that there were two possible candidates for the cook who created the pot roast. One was the mysterious, hooded parade shooter, and the other was someone who had watched the press conference and thought it would be a way to end up on the news.

I thought the second choice was just horrible. "Someone would do that?" I had asked.

All of the police people just looked at each other and then shook their heads. "Every day," someone said. "Fame is a powerful motivator, Kate."

Which was partially why they had concealed what the package

was from the media. No use in giving the cook — if that really was his motive — a sense of satisfaction.

"They aren't sure yet," I answered him. "And by the way, you can't mention that it was a pot roast to anyone else, okay?" Not like I had to worry too much about that. He didn't talk to anyone at school.

He nodded. "I won't. That's pretty weird though." He zipped his backpack shut and squinted at the clock over our mantel. "Guess I need to get going. Have a good day, Kate."

"Thanks again, Justin."

"I'll be back around two thirty or so."

He left.

Sometimes it still weirded me out how much we talked now.

Mom came into the living room as Justin left. She looked exhausted, and she was massaging the sides of her forehead. "Got your homework taken care of?"

I nodded. "Sure you can't stay home today, Mom?" Surely she needed a break.

She shook her head. "I wish I could, Kate. I know I'm completely booked back-to-back this morning. I'm going to check my schedule though. If I don't have very many appointments this afternoon I might have Madge move them all to next week instead and just come home early." She disappeared into her room to finish getting ready.

She and Dad both left at the same time. "Be careful," Dad said.

"Pay attention," Mom said.

"Don't answer the door," Dad said.

"But please answer the phone," Mom said.

"Stay inside and lock the doors," Dad said.

"Bye guys," I said.

They both left. I sat back down on the couch and pulled over *The Grapes of Wrath* again, but I didn't feel like reading anymore. All the words were starting to blur in front of me.

So I leaned my head back against the cushion, pulled my feet up next to me, and turned on the TV.

Almost eight o'clock on a weekday morning. I flipped through the channels and settled on an old *I Love Lucy* rerun. Lucy was yet again trying to get Ricky to let her into show business, and I half wondered what my life would be like if I married a Cuban bongo player.

Probably louder. Definitely louder than my life was right now. Detective Masterson was still quietly flipping through the paper, and I think DJ had decided he was going to try and get in a power nap because he just wasn't feeling very alert. Lolly was lounging on the floor, licking a rawhide bone. She never chewed them, she just licked them.

The show ended and another episode started. I curled up tighter and moved my head to the armrest.

My eyelids felt heavy. And my eyes felt completely dry, like I might need to invest in a humidifier soon.

I blinked to moisten them, but then just kept my eyes closed because it felt good.

The doorbell was ringing. The doorbell was ringing, and no one was going to answer it. So I walked over and opened the door.

John X stood there holding a fork in one hand and a spoon in the other. "I thought I'd join you for some meat loaf," he said in a deep, bass voice. A man in a hooded sweatshirt came up behind him, also holding utensils.

"I don't have any meat loaf," I told him.

"It's okay. We'll make some. I have a great recipe from my great-grandmother," John X said, walking into my house and into the kitchen, where a few bowls were already laid out on the counter.

"Let's see," he said, setting his fork and spoon down and rubbing his chin. "We need meat and a loaf of bread."

The man in the hooded sweatshirt got the bread for John X from the pantry. He didn't say anything. I looked at him and he smiled politely, but he still didn't say anything.

John X was looking at me. "Where's the meat?"

I opened the freezer and there was only frozen rawhide bones in there. "We don't have any," I said. "My mom hasn't been grocery shopping in a while."

John X looked around the kitchen for a few minutes. "Well, then. Do you have a dog?"

I nodded.

"I guess we found our meat then. Go ahead and call the dog in here." John X rolled up his sleeves and motioned to the hooded man. "We'll need your help too. Sometimes dogs can get a bit hard to skin."

I shook my head. "I don't want to use Lolly."

"You just said you don't have any other meat," John X in a *duh* tone of voice. "We have to use the dog."

"No, we don't. We can go to the store."

The hooded man started to look impatient.

"Look, just call the dog in here," John X snapped. "Call the dog or we'll use you instead."

I started crying. "Why can't we just go out to eat?" I asked. "Why do we have to eat Lolly or me?"

"That's it," John X said, grabbing my arm. "Get a knife," he instructed the hooded man. "We'll use her leg. She's got more meat there than anywhere else."

I started screaming and tried to run, but John X had a firm grip on my arms.

"Kate," he said sharply over my screams. "Kate!"

I screamed all the louder.

"Kate!"

Suddenly, I was being jerked up and shaken. I blinked awake. Detective Masterson was gripping me by both arms, shaking me and yelling, "Kate! Kate!"

The room started to settle into place. *The Price Is Right* was on the TV. Lolly was licking my toes.

Detective Masterson looked scared. He set me down on the couch and exhaled, rubbing his hands together.

I was shaking uncontrollably and tears were pouring down my face.

"Are you okay?" he asked, sitting down beside me and rubbing my shoulders.

"What happened?" I asked.

"You started screaming. You were sleeping, and you just started screaming." He shook his head. "Then you wouldn't snap out of it." He looked over at me. "Are you okay?"

I sniffed and tried to stop the torrent of tears. "He wanted to make meat loaf using me," I hiccupped.

"John X?" Detective Masterson asked quietly.

I nodded, lifting a shaking hand to wipe my cheeks. Lolly was now laying on my feet.

Detective Masterson sighed and rubbed his eyes. "Well, that wouldn't have been too tasty," he said, smiling shortly. "You're kind of skin and bones, Kate."

"He was going to use my leg."

"That makes more sense." He smiled again at me and took a deep breath. "Sheesh, kid. You scared the daylights out of me."

I looked around. "Where's DJ?"

The detective brushed a hand nonchalantly. "That guy could sleep through a root canal. I'm worried about you. Kate, I don't think you should take the sketch artist job."

I got the tears to stop and rubbed my cheeks. "Why?"

"Look at you. You can't sleep, you hardly eat anything anymore. You won't go to school." He shrugged. "You are extremely talented, and we'll be losing a huge asset to the team, but you can't handle this."

Now I just sounded weak. There were hundreds of people out there who made their living doing far more dangerous things than criminal sketches. You never heard of any of them having nervous breakdowns.

I'd never had a nervous breakdown, but I wondered if the not sleeping and hardly being able to eat was part of one.

Mom would probably know the answer to that.

Not that I would ask her.

That would be about as bright as giving Allison Northing a megaphone for Christmas. No good could come from it. Sort of like when Grandma Carter got my dad the *Complete Guide to Engineer Jokes, Riddles, and Slap-Knees* for his birthday about five years ago. He still drags that thing out every so often.

Mom and I still don't find any of the jokes very slap-kneeish. And what's with that word anyway? I wasn't aware that you could just randomly turn verbs into nouns.

"I'll keep thinking on it," I said to Detective Masterson. "Maybe I won't take the job, maybe I will. We'll just have to see."

He gave me a long look before nodding. "Okay."

Chapter Seventeen

THE WEEK WENT BY VERY SLOWLY. JUSTIN CAME EVERY morning at seven to pick up my homework and every afternoon before three to deliver it. Most of the days he didn't stay and chat.

There had been no new leads on the parade shooter. The cops still had a couple of guys watching the grocery store in Ballwin, but no one resembling the man at the parade had been there in the last two weeks.

Detective Masterson and DJ tried to be encouraging, but I could tell that they were starting to get sick of this.

Mom and Dad went to work exhausted and came home even more exhausted.

And I tried every method possible to get myself to go to sleep at night. I had Detective Masterson pick up some lavender-scented lotion at the store and tried using it before I went to bed to get me to be more tired. I tried taking that cough medicine that knocks you out, even though I wasn't coughing.

None of those seemed to work. I tossed and turned from the moment I got into bed Thursday night. I looked at the clock at one point and it was three fifteen in the morning.

I'd probably slept a whole two hours.

Finally, I gave up. I turned on my bedside lamp and dragged my sketchpad over. I'd been working on one sketch all week, and I was nearly done.

The red-haired man with a buzz cut smiled back at me from the pad, and I started working on his chin.

It was DJ.

I don't think he knew that I was sketching him. Next up was Detective Masterson and then probably my parents.

I had nothing better to do.

At three forty-five, I finished DJ's chin and pushed the pad back a few inches to get a better look at it. It looked just like him, and I was rather proud of my efforts.

I yawned and tried to decide if I could fall asleep now. Sometimes just getting a little bit of energy out seemed to help.

I tried shutting my eyes, but sleep didn't come. My brain was still working overtime. I wondered if John X's friend had somehow gotten the tip that so many people had seen him at the grocery store in Ballwin, and he'd moved on to a super Walmart or something.

Some of those had self-checkouts. You could go in, get your groceries, pay for them, and leave without anyone so much as even noticing you.

We had gotten some reports back on the pot roast. There was absolutely nothing wrong with it. It apparently had been cooked to perfection, according to some of the people down at the lab. And the note that came with it?

Zero fingerprints, zero DNA.

Not that it was a shock, but it was a little sad. I was hoping that whoever had cooked the pot roast had lost a hair in there or something.

Maybe our hooded sweatshirt friend also wore hairnets occasionally.

I wasn't going to be able to go back to sleep. I started drawing another head and shoulders shot.

Detective Masterson really did look an awful lot like Orlando Bloom. Same nose, same jawline. The only thing that was different was his hair and the slightly tougher quality in his bone structure.

I worked on the sketch until six thirty and then took a quick shower. I blow-dried my hair, added some cover-up over the increasingly dark circles under my eyes, and pulled on a pair of worn jeans and a blue T-shirt.

Justin was almost annoyingly punctual. I was just walking into the living room when he rang the doorbell. DJ answered it, yawning. "Hey," he said, letting Justin in.

"Morning, guys," Justin said. He joined DJ in yawning. "Thankfully it's Friday, right?"

I nodded, but really, my weekends weren't that much different than my weekdays now. Everything just kind of blended together. I handed him my stack of homework. "Thanks again, Justin." We were starting to sound like a broken record. He came in, said good morning, I said thank you, he said no problem, and then he left.

"No problem," he said, shoving my homework into his backpack.

Then it was his cue to leave. Instead, he sat down on the sofa.

DJ and I exchanged looks, because this was not according to schedule. Then DJ cleared his throat and left the room.

Justin looked at me. "So, have they found that guy from the parade yet?"

No offense to Justin, but you'd think this would have been fairly obvious.

"Um. No. Not yet," I said. I was still standing by the recliner, just looking at him, waiting for him to leave before I started my new morning routine. *Happy Days*, a show I'd never seen before but was apparently about life in the 50s but was made in the 70s, came on at seven. Then I watched *Friends*, watched a guy named Bobby Flay do cooking competitions, and napped during *I Love Lucy*.

So far, Detective Masterson had only had to wake me up once since Monday because I was screaming in my sleep again. But other than that, I was getting fairly decent three-hour naps in every day.

"Are you going to wait until after he's caught before you come back to school?" Justin asked, apparently staying to chat today.

I sat down in the recliner, rubbing my cheek. "I don't know," I said. I had thought about it, but not very much. What if he never was found? Did that mean I never went to school again? Would Detective Masterson and DJ have to live with us forever?

"Well, I think you should just come on back to school. What's the worst that could happen?" he asked.

I blinked as a hundred different scenarios that would fit the "worst thing that could ever happen" adjective raced through my head. Classmates could get shot, teachers could get hurt, I could put another cop in the hospital.

Justin apparently noticed the look on my face and winced, rubbing his cheek. "I, uh, I didn't mean that question, Kate."

Maybe it would be better if I didn't take the police department job. Maybe after all this was over and done with, I could get a full night's sleep, go to school like a normal sixteen-year-old, and have a nice life of homework and Crispix. I was even starting to miss my beat-up, barely working car.

I shrugged. "No big deal," I said. "But that's why I won't go back until he's caught." I hadn't elaborated on the *why* but I had a feeling that Justin got my drift.

He just nodded. "Okay, then." He stood, pulling his backpack up off the floor. "All right, I'd better get to school. Have a good day, Kate. I'll see you this afternoon."

"Thanks again, Justin." I walked him to the door.

"No problem."

I locked the door behind him, but not before poking my head outside first. It was a gorgeous day outside. And despite the trampling our front yard had gotten on the day of the pot roast fiasco, it looked like the grass would probably grow back just fine.

Thank goodness. Dad about died when he saw the yard after the barrage of uniforms left.

"What in the ..." His voice had trailed off and I knew better than asking him to finish his sentence as he stood in the front door, staring at what used to be his lawn of perfection. He'd had complete strangers coming to the door in years past, asking him what kind of fertilizer he used and how he kept his yard so green.

I closed the door and turned on *Happy Days*, though by this point I'd already missed the first few minutes of it.

Detective Masterson came in and settled in the recliner with the newspaper, like he did every morning. DJ was on the phone in the kitchen like he was every morning.

And Mom and Dad finished breakfast and left with their usual warnings like they did every morning.

I had just woken up from my nap during *I Love Lucy* when I saw Detective Masterson close his cell phone and look over at me. "Kate," he said, "time to pay another visit to the dentist."

I nodded, rubbing the lines on my cheek from the corduroy pillows. "Okay." Suddenly, I was wide awake. Maybe they caught the grocery store parade shooter! Maybe they'd run him down and I could go to school on Monday!

"And bring something to do," Detective Masterson said as I jumped off the couch and ran to my room for my shoes. "We'll probably be there a while."

"Okay!" I said.

I grabbed my shoes, changed into jeans quickly, and slapped a quick coating of mascara on. I closed my sketchpad and picked up my favorite pencil set, tucking both under my arm.

I could work on my drawings while we were at the station, since apparently we would be waiting there for a little while.

We left a few minutes later. DJ was driving over the speed limit and Detective Masterson kept looking at his cell phone.

"Did they catch him?" I asked excitedly.

"I don't know," Detective Masterson said.

"Did they see him?"

"I don't know."

"Did they at least identify him?"

He turned and looked at me. "I don't know, Kate. All they said was come down to the station right away."

"You didn't ask why?"

He shrugged. "We'll find out when we get there."

I just shook my head and looked out the window. All men were the same, my mother would have said. Any time Dad got off the phone with his side of the family, Mom would ask him what they said, what was going on with everyone, whether or not the dates for the family reunion would work for everyone this summer. And Dad would have absolutely no answers for her.

"I guess they were all fine," Dad would say.

"You didn't ask?" Mom would rant.

"I didn't think to."

We pulled up at the station and hurried inside. Deputy Slalom was sitting at his desk, and we were told to go on into his office.

I decided that you could always tell what kind of day it had been for the police station by the condition of Deputy Slalom's wardrobe.

So it kind of scared me when we walked in and his button-down shirt was completely unbuttoned, showing his white undershirt. His sleeves were rolled up past his elbows, and his tie was in a wad on the desk.

"Sit," he barked as soon as we walked in.

Definitely not good news. I sat immediately, setting my sketchpad and pencils on the floor under my chair. Detective Masterson sat in the chair beside me, and DJ stood behind us, since there wasn't another chair.

Deputy Slalom was pacing now, his shirttail flapping behind him. He was seething.

I watched him, my stomach knotting tighter each time he passed in front of me. I'd already resigned myself that this was not going to be the good news I was hoping for. Now, I was just hoping that there was a light at the end of the house arrest tunnel.

"Well," Deputy Slalom growled finally after five minutes

of pacing in front of us. He stopped behind his desk chair and gripped the sides of it. "Good news, Kate. They found the parade shooter."

He was still seething though, so I didn't bust into a happy dance just yet.

He squeezed the chair sides tighter. "And I just got off the phone with the Clayton county office."

Clayton is another suburb of St. Louis.

"It seems that our friendly and entirely *ridiculous* prison system has somehow *misplaced* a certain inmate!" Deputy Slalom shoved his chair against his desk so hard, the three framed pictures he had sitting on it fell over.

I jumped. I'd never heard so many stressed words from Deputy Slalom. At first, it didn't really register what he'd said because I was so shocked by the chair slamming and the yelling.

He'd seemed like such a docile man.

Guess not.

Detective Masterson went pale. "I'm sorry?" he said.

"Yeah! Yeah, that's all the guy from Clayton had to say!" Deputy Slalom was back to pacing. " 'I'm sorry.' I'm sorry?! Does that suddenly help things? Are we finally living in a society where all people have to do is halfway apologize, and suddenly everything is all rainbows and butterflies and Hostess snack cakes?!" He banged his fists down on the desk and this time a paperweight fell over.

I kept scooting farther and farther back in my chair. I'd spent many a time in the principal's office hearing about how being tardy to class is setting myself up on a road of failure and disappointment, but Principal Murray had never yelled like this at me.

Somehow I got the feeling that Deputy Slalom wasn't yelling at us as much as just venting to us.

He flung himself into his chair with a huff. "John X is missing," he said in a sullen, deathly quiet voice.

The room immediately felt like it shrunk six feet in every

direction. My chest got tight, my lungs had trouble expanding. I couldn't feel anything past my waist. Any joy about the parade shooter being captured vanished like the rare package of Nutter Butters in front of my dad.

"Missing," Detective Masterson repeated after a few minutes of complete silence in the room.

"Missing. Gone. Kaput. MIA." Deputy Slalom waved a wrist around while he spoke, his eyes glassy, his gaze fixed on the window. "He was in his cell for breakfast, and there was no one there by lunch."

My hands were shaking violently, and I tried to control them by weaving my fingers together so tight, my knuckles turned white.

"The clever man from Clayton said he thought it was his 'responsibility' to let me know that they'd somehow 'misplaced' John X, and if he happened to show up here in South Woodhaven Falls, could we 'please arrange a transport' back to the prison." Deputy Slalom started shaking his head.

"What did you say?" Detective Masterson said.

"I said a bunch of words that I'm not going to repeat in front of a minor." He looked over at me. "And a girl minor at that." He let his breath out for a long minute and kept looking at me. "Kate. This changes a lot."

I managed a nod, but I'm not sure how I did. My muscles felt frozen and stiff, like when it would snow a lot on the hill behind my house and Dad and I would go sledding on Mom's cookie sheets when she wasn't home, much to her dismay when she'd return.

Detective Masterson looked at me as well and reached over, patting my shoulder. "Don't panic, Kate."

He said it in the same tone he'd use if I'd burned myself cooking. If any situation was worthy of a good panicking, I would think that this one would be it.

DJ had been awfully quiet behind us. I looked over, and he was standing there with his arms crossed over his chest, jaw muscles set, eyes glaring.

Maybe it was better that he wasn't talking.

Deputy Slalom took another deep breath and simply shook his head.

Right then, his secretary came in and gave him a manila folder. She looked at me and gave me a sad smile before she left.

He opened the folder and nodded at the contents. "Kate, you're going into official witness protection."

I thought I was in official witness protection. I opened my mouth to ask.

"And not just at your house with a couple of cops there." He peered over at Detective Masterson. "You're going with her."

The detective nodded. "Yes, sir."

"And Kirkpatrick?"

DJ finally spoke. "Yes, sir?" His voice was hard.

"You're staying here. I'll need all the manpower I can get. Kate, you and your parents are being shipped to an undisclosed location in the next four hours." He waved at his secretary through the window facing the room filled with cubicles, and she stood from her desk, walked over, and poked her head into the office.

"Yes, sir?"

"Have a car go pick up Kate's parents." He looked at me. "I assume they are both working?"

I nodded.

He looked back at his secretary. "The info is all in their folders. I want them back here in thirty minutes."

She nodded. "Yes, sir." She closed the door and walked back to her desk.

Deputy Slalom looked back at me. "Kate, when your parents get here, you'll have one hour to pack. Pack lightly and pack the essentials."

"Where are we going?" I asked.

He started shaking his head. "I can't tell you that." He squinted at the clock. It was almost one in the afternoon. "You will be headed to your location by three. Is that understood?" Then he looked at Detective Masterson. "I want confirmation that you are there by five tonight."

I could see a muscle jumping in Detective Masterson's cheek. He nodded stiffly. "Yes, sir."

"Kate, you are not to take any cell phones, computers, or whatever the latest gadget that starts with *i* is. No communication devices at all. Anything that could be traced to you, I want left here. Is that understood?"

I nodded.

He picked up the phone on his desk and started dialing. I sat there, numb, my fingers still woven together.

"Daniels? It's Slalom. I need you to get a forensics team over to Clayton and see if they can't find how in the blazes a level-four criminal escaped from there without anyone seeing him." Deputy Slalom listened for a minute. "Thanks." Then he slammed the phone down.

"I'm going to get any and every picture of John X that we have out there circulating. If he so much as even peeks out of his little gopher hole, I want someone there to slam him over the head with a mallet and some handcuffs. And no way in ..." He looked at me briefly. "No way in *heck* am I letting him go back to Clayton. Fool me once, shame on you. They aren't fooling me twice."

I was assuming that Deputy Slalom had been referring to the old arcade game where you had to whack the little groundhogs on their heads when they popped out of the holes before they went back in.

I was never very good at that game.

Thirty minutes later, almost to the second, both of my parents ran in, looking panicked.

"Kate!" my dad shouted when he saw me. "What happened? Are you okay? Did they catch the parade shooter?"

Apparently, no one had informed my parents why a policeman had demanded that they go with him in a squad car in the middle of the day.

Detective Masterson stood and offered my mom his chair. Deputy Slalom had spent the last few minutes before they got here trying to get the media relations guy to send out bulletins about John X to all the news stations in and around Missouri.

"I want his picture as far as he can drive in one day, you got that? And at every airport, bus station, and train depot around." Then he'd slammed down his phone so hard it probably left a resounding ring in the media guy's ear.

I was starting to worry about the structural integrity of his desk with the beating it was taking today.

Mom sat down in Detective Masterson's vacated chair and reached over for me. "Are you okay?" she asked, smoothing my hair away from my face.

"What is going on here?" Dad demanded.

Deputy Slalom was back to shaking his head. "They caught the parade shooter."

"Oh yay!" Mom said.

"Yeah. Yay. And then the idiots down at the Clayton prison seemed to have somehow 'misplaced' our friend John X."

I immediately jumped up out of my chair so Dad could drop into it, since he didn't look like he'd be able to stand for much longer.

Both he and my mom just stared at the deputy.

"They what?" Dad finally said.

Another slam on the desk, which made both Mom and Dad jump. "Look, I don't have the strength to tell it again," Deputy Slalom said, almost growling as he looked around the room. "Kent, tell them what's going on."

In short, precise sentences, Detective Masterson quietly informed Mom and Dad of the situation. "So, the four of us are going to be leaving in the next two hours for an undisclosed location," he finished.

Mom sat there, mouth open.

Dad jumped up from the chair and started pacing back and forth behind it, in front of DJ.

I stood quietly against the window.

"Obviously, our primary concern is for Kate's safety," Detective Masterson said to Dad. "So, we need you guys to go home and pack only the essentials. No cell phones, computers, or any other communication device that could trace someone back to Kate."

"What about our family?" Mom started fretting. "Our son, Mike. He's in school. What am I supposed to tell him? What about my work?"

"What about our dog?" I asked.

"How often do you talk to your son?" Deputy Slalom asked Mom.

We all just looked at Mom, wondering if she'd actually admit how little she talked to him. She sighed and shrugged. "It varies."

It did vary. It varied on how often Mike needed something.

"Don't tell him anything then," Deputy Slalom said. "Here's the thing, Mrs. Carter. I don't want another person outside of these four walls to know where Kate is, whether that means lying your tail off to your work or your son."

Mom nodded and I saw the tears building.

Dad must've seen them too, because he reached down and put both hands on her shoulders. "We'll tell work that we got offered the use of a vacation house and we decided to take it. Considering everything that has happened, I don't think anyone's going to doubt our need of a good vacation."

Mom nodded again and sniffed. "And Mike?" she asked quietly.

Dad sighed. "We'll tell him we won't be able to answer our phones for a while and if he needs to get ahold of us to have him call ..." Dad's voice trailed off and he looked at Deputy Slalom. "I guess giving him Kent's number wouldn't be the wisest, would it?"

"Tell him to call your friend Gene," Deputy Slalom said. He tapped a nameplate I hadn't noticed before on his desk. It was gold and engraved.

Deputy Gene Slalom.

Dad nodded. Mom nodded. Detective Masterson nodded.

I was too busy feeling sorry that the deputy had to go through life with a name like Gene Slalom to nod. No wonder he went into law enforcement.

"Make your calls," Deputy Slalom said. "And then you've got an hour to pack. I want every one of you gone by three."

"And Lolly?" I asked.

Deputy Slalom sighed. "What kind of dog is she?"

"Lab, sir."

He sighed harder. "My wife and I will take her for a few days."

Mom immediately pulled out her cell phone and pushed the speed dial. She waited for a while, her expression growing bleaker and bleaker with each passing second. "Hi, honey," she said, finally, and I could hear her holding back the tears as she talked. "It's Mom. We're going on something of a last-minute vacation and our cell phones won't work there, so if you need something, call our friend Gene at 555 – 8711." She paused. "Love you, Mike."

Dad was on the phone with his work. "We got offered a fabulous vacation rental for a little while, and we think that we of all people deserve a vacation," he said. "My cell won't work, so just hold all my calls and I'll return them when I get back."

I opened my cell phone and looked at it. Who did I need to call? Who did I want to call?

I sent Maddy a text message. *We are going out of town for a few days. No cell reception. Talk later.*

Then I called Justin. It was almost two, which meant last period had started a little over thirty minutes ago. I was expecting his voicemail.

Just so I could tell him not to bother with the homework.

"Hi, Kate," he answered.

I frowned at the phone. "Justin?"

"Yeah?"

"Why are you answering your phone?"

He paused. "Um. You called me on it."

"No, I know, but aren't you in school?"

"I've got study hall the last period. I went out to the hallway."

I shrugged. "Oh."

"So, uh, did you need something?"

Mom was calling her secretary, Madge, to tell her to hold all of her appointments.

"Yeah, Justin," I said, quietly. "I need you to not pick up my homework anymore. You see, there was this great vacation house that opened up, and Mom and Dad decided we needed a little bit of family time away from everything. And since I wasn't going to school anyway ..." I let my voice trail off. "But thanks for helping me out these last few weeks."

I got ready to hang up.

"Wait, wait," he said. "You're just leaving?"

"Yeah."

"Just like that?"

"Just like that," I said. It didn't seem like the people on the other end of Mom and Dad's calls were having this much trouble believing them. I must not have been a very good liar.

Justin paused like he didn't believe me and he had more questions, but I jumped in before he could start. "Anyway, good to talk to you, thanks for everything, bye!"

I closed my phone quickly, feeling bad for hanging up on him, but I would have felt worse if I'd let something slip.

Twenty minutes later, I was throwing as many belongings as I could into my suitcase that I hadn't used in two years.

I didn't even remember what my suitcase looked like. Dad had to get it out of the garage for me because I couldn't find it.

"Maybe we need to go on 'vacations' more often," Dad said, rolling his eyes.

We both knew why we hadn't gone anywhere for so long. Mom couldn't stand the thought of us going on a family vacation without Mike.

And Mike was never here.

So we never went.

I put in socks, T-shirts, long sleeves, jeans, and shorts, just so I was prepared for any type of weather, though if we were driving and Deputy Slalom was planning on us getting there — wherever there was — by five, then we weren't going very far away.

I grabbed a few books, found a couple of DVDs that I hadn't seen in a while to throw in there, and reached over for my sketchpad.

It wasn't on my desk.

Actually, it wasn't anywhere in my room.

"Mom, have you seen my sketchpad?" I asked her as she ran down the hall, hauling an armload of whites that were fresh from the dryer.

She shook her head. "Sorry, Katie-Kin. Did you check the family room?" She disappeared into her bedroom. I could see Dad in there packing ammunition beside his clothing.

I looked in the living room, the kitchen, and had DJ go look in the black Tahoe. Detective Masterson was home packing, and he would bring back the car we were going to take.

"You can't be too careful," he'd said.

DJ came back inside shaking his head. "Sorry, Kate. It's not there." He had a helpless look on his face, and he'd had it on there since we'd gotten back to my house.

I figured he was probably wishing he was coming with us. He'd spent the past three weeks living with us, after all.

"I'm sorry you aren't coming with us," I said.

He just nodded at me. "Me too."

I went back to my room to finish packing. Suddenly I remembered where my sketchbook was. I'd left it underneath my chair in Deputy Slalom's office.

I heard Detective Masterson come into our house then. He stuck his head in my room. "Time to go, Kate."

"I left my sketchpad and pencils at the station," I told him.

He shrugged. "We don't have time to stop for it. I'm sorry, Kate. Do you have another one you can bring?"

I had one from last summer that still had a few empty pages in it. I sighed and packed that one instead alongside a bunch of pencils that weren't my favorite brand, but weren't awful.

Detective Masterson had brought a white GMC Yukon and parked it in the garage. We quietly piled into it while the garage door was still closed. DJ was still at our house when we left.

"Hope we see you again soon," I said as we climbed into the Yukon.

He nodded. "Drive safely." He closed my door and walked quickly back inside, shutting the door behind him. The goal was to leave as unnoticed as possible. There was no telling whether there were still camera crews watching my house.

Detective Masterson instructed all of us to duck down in our seats for the time being. He wanted whoever was watching — if anyone was watching — to think that he'd driven up alone and left alone. I think Dad had the hardest seat to do that since he was sitting in the passenger seat.

Mom and I laid down on the backseat. All of our bags were behind us and I started thinking about where we were going. Was it a hotel? A cabin? I'd seen movies where the people had to be put in protective custody, but I'd never ever thought it would happen to me.

Finally, Detective Masterson said we could sit up again. We were on the highway, headed west.

"Can you tell us where we're going now?" I asked.

He shook his head. "You'll be able to tell the basic area soon, but it's best if you don't know details, Kate."

"Is it a hotel?"

"I can't tell you."

I looked out the window. "Is it a camping site?"

"Kate," he said, looking at me in the rearview mirror. "No details, kid. Sorry. You'll find out soon enough."

"Detective Masterson?"

He sighed. "Yes, Kate?"

"Can you turn on the radio?"

He flipped it on and it was tuned to the local country station, and I had to wonder about the detective's musical tastes. This wasn't cool country like Rascal Flatts.

This was old-school country, like whatever the guy's name was who had the long, gray hair and wore old blankets around.

Dad started humming along and settled back in his chair contentedly. "See? This was the era of good music."

"Agreed," Detective Masterson said.

I looked at my mom, who was rolling her eyes. Mom tends to be very modern-day with her musical choices. She worked out to the Black Eyed Peas and Justin Timberlake.

I told Maddy that and she's thought my mom was the coolest mom ever since then. Apparently, her mom doesn't work out and the only music she ever listens to is the commercial medleys between talk show hosts.

Mom always said that the eighties were a period of horrific hairstyles and much-too-short shorts for men, so why in the world did anyone assume that those same people who created those styles could create quality music? Her case in point was Madonna, but I would have used someone like Boy George.

He was just plain weird.

Two hours later, we were passing the signs for Columbia, Missouri, when Detective Masterson put his blinker on and exited the freeway.

I perked up. I'd been staring out the window without really watching the scenery, trying to block out the old-timer country music.

We were going to Columbia?

He kept driving through the town and turned right on a tiny two-lane road that went on and on for miles. All around us were trees, hills, and more trees. And the trees got thicker the farther we drove.

Detective Masterson made several more turns and finally

stopped in front of a tiny house in the middle of a clearing that was pretty much in the middle of a forest.

"Welcome to your hopefully temporary home," Detective Masterson said, putting the Yukon in park and turning off the engine.

The house looked creepy. I stared at it through the windshield. It was small and square and looked like it could have been the hideout for the Unabomber at one point.

Everyone climbed out, and I stepped out of the car onto a carpet of pine needles. The trees were ginormous and I wondered at what point the little house had last seen daylight. Between the thick trees, hardly any sun made it through to the ground.

Birds were chirping, but other than that, it was totally silent.

I shivered, creeped out again.

Dad picked up his and Mom's suitcases, and Detective Masterson grabbed his and mine before heading up to the front porch of the house. He unlocked the front door, and it squealed in protest as it opened.

"Come on in," he said, leading the way and flicking on lights as he went.

The house was tiny. There was a living room and kitchen directly off the front door. Then a short hallway and three miniature bedrooms. Orange shag carpeting covered everything but the kitchen. Detective Masterson set my suitcase on the creaky twin bed in the last bedroom. "Might as well get comfortable, Kate."

I looked around the room. Everything had dark wood paneling covering it, even the closet doors. The bedspread on the bed was an ivory-colored quilt. There was a short dresser in the room and no other furniture.

I walked back into the family room, where Detective Masterson was talking quietly on his cell phone.

"Yes, sir. Yes, sir." He saw me come in and waved to me. "I'll tell her, sir. All right. Bye." He closed the phone, pocketed it, and looked at me. "I need to show you something that this house has." He pointed to the kitchen, and I followed him in there.

The kitchen was old. Old orange linoleum, old appliances, old dark wood paneling everywhere.

Detective Masterson knelt down in front of the sink. "See this?" he pointed up under the countertop. I bent over.

A small white button was there.

"Yeah," I said.

"That's a silent alarm. There's one in every bedroom, two in here and two in the living room. If you push that button, a team from the FBI will be here in the next four and a half minutes."

I nodded. "Okay."

"If anything feels even off to you, you come find me. If you can't find me for whatever reason, you push that button. Got it?" He was looking at me very seriously.

I nodded again. "Got it."

"I'll show you where all the buttons are."

He took me on a tour around the house and pointed out every hidden button. I never would have seen them if they hadn't been pointed out to me.

"How often do you guys use this house?" I asked.

"This is the first time our department's ever had to use it," Detective Masterson said when we got back into the living room. "But it's open to all police and FBI in the Missouri area."

"And when was the last time someone thought about updating it?" I asked, poking at one of the yellowing lace curtains over the front window.

He grinned. "You don't like it?" He looked around, smiling. "I guess it could use a little sprucing. Hopefully we won't be here long enough to pull out the home décor books though. And really, it is pretty up to date." He pointed to the window. "All the glass in here? Bulletproof. And the alarm system, of course. And there's a sensor that tracks body heat that is within the five miles surrounding this place. All those gadgets are in my room."

"What about bears?" I asked.

"What about them?"

"Do they come close to the house?"

He shrugged. "They've never hurt anyone if they do."

Not quite the answer I was looking for. I'd seen a documentary on TV one time about a man who tamed bears and fed them on his land, and he was trying to tell the world that they really were just nice, cuddly creatures, but I had a hard time believing him.

Sort of like when people have told me that rats make good pets. I just don't believe them. Rats are disgusting.

I sat down on the olive green and orange-striped couch and looked at the TV. It had a dial on it.

Dad and Mom came out into the living room then.

"Wow, I haven't seen a TV like that since college," Dad said, excitedly. He reached over and twisted a knob, and the TV blinked a few times and then came on to pure static.

"Yeah, about the TV," Detective Masterson said. "I think since we are so thick into these trees, only a few channels make it through."

Dad twisted the knob around, and Mom joined me on the couch.

A couple of minutes later, a baseball game flickered through the static. Dad was overjoyed.

"Look at this, Claire!" he said, sitting down next to Mom. "Kate, this was what TV was for us when we were little kids. None of this flatscreen HD madness. Just good old-fashioned rabbit ears."

"Mm-hmm," I said. I was a little distracted by the pitcher's head moving from right to left across the screen without bringing his body with it.

I got up from the couch and went to get my sketchbook. The only place to draw was on the kitchen table, so I sat down and pulled out my rubber-banded pencils.

Detective Masterson was standing in the kitchen, checking out the contents in the fridge.

"No food?" I asked.

"Oh, there's food. The guys in Columbia stocked it for us before we got here." He pulled out a big jug of chocolate milk. "Want a glass?"

I couldn't even remember the last time I had chocolate milk. Probably since before Mom's big health kick. I started nodding.

He poured two glasses and then sat down at the table with me, passing my cup over.

"What are you working on?" he asked.

I shrugged. I had been working on his face, but I'd left that sketchbook in Deputy Slalom's office. "I don't know," I said. Maybe I'd draw my parents now. Or the pitcher with the wavy head.

"So, I got you something," he said. "Before I knew we were coming here, but I did pack it in my suitcase, so hang on a second."

He disappeared down the hallway and came back with a thin box. Sitting back down at the table, he passed it over to me.

NIV Bible.

I frowned. It seemed like the box holding the Bible might be spell-checked more carefully. What in the world was a "Niv"?

"You don't have to read it," he said, watching my face. "I just thought with some of the questions you've been asking me, and your mom trying to get you guys to go to church more, that you might need a Bible."

"Thanks," I said. "What's a 'niv'?"

"A niv?" he parroted confusedly and then looked at the box. "Oh! NIV? That means New International Version."

"Oh," I said. I opened the box and the Bible was thin and on the smaller side, covered in soft, buttery-smooth brown leather.

It was nothing like the incredibly bulky and heavy Bibles I'd seen at South Woodhaven Falls First Baptist.

"Thanks, Detective Masterson," I said, smiling at him.

"You're welcome. And I would start in Luke, by the way," he said. "This isn't like a normal book where you start at the beginning and work your way through."

I nodded.

Dad stood up. "Okay, his head is making me crazy," he said, fiddling with the rabbit ears on the back of the TV.

Now the pitcher's head was standing still, but his body was moving back and forth.

"HD TV is looking pretty good right now, huh, sweetie?" Mom said, and I could hear the mocking grin in her voice.

It could be a long time in this tiny house.

Chapter Eighteen

FIVE DAYS PASSED VERY SLOWLY. BY THE END OF THE SECOND day, Dad had rigged an entire coat hanger system over the TV, and we then had about fifteen more channels than we originally had and no more fuzzy heads.

Mom had paced the short length from the front living room window to the back kitchen window two hundred and seventeen times. Then she started doing lunges from the back window to the front window.

Detective Masterson spent most of the time reading. I'd discovered he was a Clive Cussler fan. The only thing I knew about Clive Cussler was that the movie *Sahara* with Matthew McConaughey was based on one of his books.

I wasn't really a Matthew McConaughey fan. He was shirtless too much of the time.

I alternated between working on pictures of Mom and Dad while munching on Chips Ahoy and taking naps, since I still wasn't sleeping at night.

The house was starting to feel smaller and smaller.

Wednesday morning at two fifteen, I was still staring up at the ceiling with bleary eyes. When we'd first gotten there, the room had been pitch black at night, because there weren't any streetlights like at home to give a comforting glow to the room.

After the first night of no sleeping, Detective Masterson handed me a night-light to plug in.

I felt like a wimp for needing a night-light to sleep. I was, after all, sixteen years old, and night-lights were typically used with what? Two-year-olds?

Next thing I knew, I'd be asking for a blanket and a binky.

The night-light helped though. Obviously I still wasn't sleeping, but at least I wasn't laying in bed with my heart pounding wondering if there was someone in my closet or not.

I slept with my closet doors open too.

I looked at the clock again. Two seventeen.

Yay. Two whole minutes had passed.

Sighing, I reached over for the ancient Tiffany-style bedside lamp and turned it on, blinking into the sudden burst of light. My eyes felt raw and dried out, sort of like week-old grapes that probably just needed to be tossed.

The Bible that Detective Masterson had given me was laying on the bedside table. I hadn't read anything in it so far.

Start in Luke, he'd said.

I picked it up and opened it. The pages were super thin, like tissue paper. Maybe owning a Bible wasn't a good idea for someone like me who tended to accidentally rip things.

I turned the first pages until I got to the table of contents and found the listing for Luke. Page 847.

The Bible was a lot bigger than I'd figured it was.

I flipped over carefully and ended up in a section called Psalms on my way over to Luke.

There were a lot of chapters in Psalms. I was looking at Psalm 112 and there were still a bunch after it.

One line caught my eye. "They will have no fear of bad news; their hearts are steadfast, trusting in the LORD."

I wasn't sure who "they" were, but I found myself wishing that I could be like them. You know, the whole not fearing bad news.

At this point, my life was all about fear.

I read a little further in the Psalm and some of it sounded like the songs we'd sung at church last Sunday.

I wondered what it would be like to be like Justin or Detective Masterson. Both of them seemed so set that everything that was happening was God's plan. And for some reason, that made everything okay.

Everything was not okay, though. I'd already been shot at once, and now the guy who I put in prison was likely out there looking for me.

I shivered and looked at the closed blinds covering the bulletproof window. My life had been reduced to a tiny house in the middle of the woods of Missouri.

I spent the next three hours reading in the Psalms. By the time I reached over to turn off the bedside lamp to try and get a few more hours of sleep, I could hear the birds starting their morning chirping.

I slept until almost eight, which was really good for me. I walked out into the living room after I brushed my teeth and found Mom and Dad pulling on their sneakers.

"Morning, Katie-Kin. We're going for a quick walk," Mom said, doing a couple of stretches. "Want to come with us?"

I watched Mom do a few lunges and shook my head, yawning. I might be going stir-crazy, but I wasn't about to go power walking with Mom. Mom took her walks far too seriously.

I was actually amazed that Dad was going to go with her. He mocked her mercilessly about how she walked.

He must be really bored.

"No, thanks," I said. "Have fun." I sat down on the couch.

"We'll be back soon," Mom said, kissing the top of my head.

"I'll tell Kent we're leaving," Dad said.

I looked around. "Where is he?"

He shrugged. "Something about the motion sensor. I think he's working on it in the shed out back."

They left and I went to pour a bowl of Cocoa Puffs, one of the many contraband items in our house that was luckily in plenty of supply here. Detective Masterson walked in as I was pouring the milk over them, listening to the happy sounds of chocolate snapping.

"Good morning, Kate," he said, backhanding his forehead and reaching for a bottle of water from the fridge.

"Hot outside?"

"Stuffy in the shed," he said after gulping half the bottle. "Anyway, I've got to finish working on this thing." He unclipped his cell phone and set it beside me on the table. "If you need anything or anything even seems off, push 4 – 6 – 3. That will buzz my pager."

I nodded. "Okay."

"It shouldn't take me too long. And I'm just behind the house."

I nodded again. "Okay."

"Have a good breakfast."

He left and the house suddenly felt very quiet.

Quiet, dark, and small.

I ate my Cocoa Puffs in crunching silence, reading the back of the box as I ate. Apparently, Toucan Sam had a friend who was crazy for this cereal.

I put my bowl in the sink when I finished and found my sketchbook. My parents' heads were coming along, but I wasn't quite done yet.

I sat down on the couch.

Nothing like an orange and olive green–striped couch sitting on orange carpeting and surrounded by dark wood paneling to get the inspiration rolling.

I stared at my parents' half-finished heads for about fifteen minutes before I finally just flipped the page over and started drawing something else.

Last night, one of the Psalm chapters, the first one I think, had mentioned something about someone sitting under a tree or being like a tree or something like that. That was one of the last ones I read, so it was a little fuzzy to me. But looking out the front window and seeing just a mesh of trees made me think of it.

I usually liked to stick to people but I started sketching the forest. I drew the window frame I was looking through, complete with the wood paneling on the sides of it. Then, through the window, I drew the trees.

The sound of Detective Masterson's phone ringing startled me and I jumped, my pencil making the limbs on one tree look more abstract than real.

I walked over to the table and looked at the cell. He had one of those phones that rang and vibrated at the same time, so it was jangling and turning in a circle on the table.

He hadn't told me what to do if his phone rang.

I picked it up and looked at the screen.

Slalom.

I should probably answer it if it was the deputy calling.

"Hello?" I said, my voice all mousy. I hated how I seemed to always talk an octave higher on the phone.

"Who is this?" Deputy Slalom demanded.

"Um. Kate, sir. Kate Carter."

"Kate, why are you answering Kent's phone?"

"Um. Because he's out working in the shed." Now, not only was I talking an octave higher, I was stuttering and a tattletale.

Today was going to be a great day.

"Get him. NOW!"

I nearly dropped the phone when he yelled. "Uh, yes, sir," I managed, fumbling with the phone and running for the front door. My stomach was flip-flopping like I had a dozen or so wide-mouthed bass swimming around in there.

Maybe they'd caught John X!

I shoved my feet in some flip-flops and ran out the front door, leaving it slightly ajar, and onto the porch. The birds were singing, there was a slight breeze, and the sun was shining through the trees in small patches all over the pine-needle-blanketed clearing.

The shed was in the back. I hadn't been to the back yet since I was pretty content to stay inside, all things considered.

"Did you find him?" Deputy Slalom barked at me.

"Uh, not yet, sir."

"Good grief, Kate, the house is tinier than my aunt Gladys' kitchen! Find him now!"

"Yes, sir. Right away, sir."

I tripped over the natural landscape and found myself thankful for the manicured lawn Dad cared so much about. I didn't even have to worry about stubbing my toe in his grass.

Not like I was ever allowed to walk on it.

I finally saw the shed a few feet back from the house and I hurried as quickly as I could toward it, phone smashed to my ear, trying to avoid all the fallen branches, rocks, and probably snake holes around.

I had one thing in common with Indiana Jones, and that was that we both hated snakes. Other than that, we were total opposites.

It was my goal to lead my life in relative obscurity.

Which obviously was not happening right now.

I looked up at the shed and saw someone coming out of it, closing both the doors behind him.

It was DJ.

"DJ!" I shouted, waving and smiling.

"DJ?" Deputy Slalom yelled in my ear.

"Hi!" I said.

He waved back and started walking in my direction.

"Kate! Listen to me — run! Get as far away from DJ as you can!" Deputy Slalom yelled.

I stopped about halfway between the house and the shed, frowning. "What?" I said. "It's DJ. The guy from your police force?"

"Kate, get in the house! Get back in the house *now*!"

I didn't try to argue with him, but I couldn't help thinking how ridiculous it was for me to be running back to the house when I'd just waved at DJ.

DJ had lived with us for the last month. What did Deputy Slalom think he'd do? Hug me in greeting?

"Kate!" DJ yelled behind me, and I could hear him crashing through the brush. "Kate, hold on!"

I tripped up the front steps and into the front door, closing it and locking it behind me right as DJ rammed into it, grabbing the knob. "Kate!" he shouted again.

What if DJ had news about John X? What if he knew something and had driven all the way out here to tell us?

"Are you in the house?" Deputy Slalom was still yelling at me.

My heart was pounding. I just stared at DJ through the window on the front door. "Yes, sir."

"Do not open that door, Kate. Do you hear me? Do *not* open that door!"

DJ pounded on the door. "Open the door, Kate! Don't listen to him!"

"Deputy, what — ?"

"You left your sketchbook here," Deputy Slalom shouted.

I went into the kitchen to get away from DJ's pounding on the door. "Okay."

"You left your sketchbook here and one of the guys we brought up from St. Louis started looking through it."

A sketchbook isn't the same thing as a journal, but for me, it can be. I felt myself getting a little offended. "He what?"

"He looked through it and saw the picture you did of DJ."

My heart started beating a little faster. I watched as DJ paced the front porch, staring into the house, shouting at me.

"Open the door, Kate!"

"Kate. He recognized him. From a case about four years ago."

Surely Deputy Slalom meant that DJ had worked on the case. He must have worked in St. Louis.

I couldn't get a full breath into my lungs. They felt cramped, like there suddenly wasn't enough room in my rib cage.

"Kate, a man matching DJ's exact description was an accomplice in John X's first murder."

And just like that, my heart stopped pounding. I sank to the kitchen chair, shock making it impossible for my kneecaps to hold the standing position.

"But he ... how ...?"

"We hired him exactly three and a half years ago. He had no police record, we didn't know anything about any of this. But the cop from St. Louis brought up the case records from the first murder." Deputy Slalom sighed and I could picture him rubbing his forehead. "Kate, it's him. I don't know the whys and I really don't understand the hows, but it's him."

"Kate! Open the door!" DJ yelled, pounding on the front window.

I looked at him, and the fear took over. I shook from head to toe. DJ? The same guy who slept outside my room on an air mattress for the last four weeks? The guy who panicked when Officer DeWeise was shot, the guy who tried to make me laugh when he could tell I was getting freaked out?

He, of all people, was working with the man who was trying to kill me?

DJ looked and sounded angry. His eyes were bloodshot, his face was bright red, and he was yelling constantly.

I started worrying about my mom and dad. And Detective Masterson. I'd seen DJ coming out of the shed. What if he'd killed Detective Masterson and my parents?

I started shaking harder. Tears were gathering in the corners of my eyes, and I felt like all of my muscles had turned to overcooked noodles.

"Stay on the phone with me, Kate," Deputy Slalom said. "I've got the FBI headed your direction."

"Kate! Kate!" DJ started banging both fists on the window, screaming at the top of his lungs. "Kate!"

I don't think I even realized what happened at first.

One minute I was holding the phone, Deputy Slalom talking in my ear about how the FBI was on the way, the next minute the phone was gone and I was face-to-face with a man whose face I knew better than my own.

"Hello, Kate Carter from South Woodhaven Falls."

It was John X.

Chapter Nineteen

I COULD ONLY ASSUME THAT MY CENTRAL NERVOUS SYSTEM had shut down, because for some reason I was very calm right then. The man I'd been having nightmares about for weeks was standing right in front of me closing Detective Masterson's phone and smiling smugly.

And I just sat there. I didn't scream. I didn't faint.

I didn't even twitch.

DJ, meanwhile, was continuing to pound on the door, the window, the siding on the house, yelling at the top of his lungs. "Kate! Kate!"

John X ignored him. Instead, he pulled out the chair to my right and sat down at the table with me, pushing the detective's cell phone to the other side of it.

"So, Kate Carter," he said.

His voice was different than I'd imagined it. It wasn't scarily deep. It was cultured, almost. Precise.

I just looked at him. He was, all things considered, a very nice-looking man. A strong jawline, high cheekbones. And unlike the thin-lipped, beady-eyed crooks like I'd always imagined, John X actually had a nice smile and really pretty brown eyes. He wasn't too tall and he wasn't too short. And he was dressed fairly stylishly — straight-cut jeans, a collared Polo shirt.

No wonder he'd targeted women. It was difficult to think of the man in front of me committing a moving traffic violation, much less murder.

I didn't say anything.

He knit his fingers together on the table and looked over at me. "So, you've made things a little difficult for me lately," he said.

I kept thinking about the panic buttons Detective Masterson had told me about. If only I could get up nonchalantly and push one of the buttons.

"KATE!" DJ yelled.

John X sighed and looked out the window. "Your friend is a slow learner."

"Apparently, he's your friend too," I said quietly, surprising myself with the sound of my voice.

John X's mouth curled in a small smile. "Is that what your friendly deputy just told you?"

I shrugged but inside I was worried. If he knew I was talking to Deputy Slalom, then he knew that it was only a matter of time before the FBI got here.

So why was he just sitting at the dining room table with me? Why hadn't he killed me and moved on before he got caught again?

Four and a half minutes, that's what Detective Masterson had told me. It would take the FBI four and a half minutes to get here.

It had been two since I'd talked to the deputy and he'd said they were on their way.

"You're quite young," John X said, looking at me, sounding almost surprised. "How old are you?"

"Sixteen."

"I knew you were still in high school, but I wasn't expecting ... well, when does life really go by your expectations, though, right?" He sat up straighter. "Such a shame. I bet you were going to be the shining star of the South Woodhaven Falls police force, hmm?"

My nerves were back at his use of the past tense in referring to me. I clasped my hands together to keep from shaking. I kept thinking about the Psalm I read last night. The "they" who had no reason to fear.

I had reason to fear.

It had been three minutes. I only needed another minute and a half.

I sat quietly and he watched me, leaning back in his chair. The only sound was DJ's occasional yell.

"How come you aren't letting him in?" I asked finally.

"How come you aren't?" he asked me.

"Because I heard he was with you."

"Interesting," John X said, rubbing his chin. "Because I've been hearing different reports about little Darren there." He looked over at DJ, who was staring through the window, visibly seething. "Consciences can be deadly things."

I frowned. "So DJ didn't help you kill the first lady?"

John X snapped his gaze back to me. "Oh, no. He did. He just didn't adapt as well to life after the murder. Some people just can't face who they really are, you know?"

Dad had told me that exact phrase once during one of his infamous Kate-should-become-an-engineer talks. I'd made a comment that I wasn't sure I wanted to be an engineer and Dad had only said, "Well. Some people can't face who they really are until college. You'll get there, Kate. You'll get there."

Detective Masterson believed in a whole "plan" type of life where everything was God's plan.

Was this God's plan? Me accidentally drawing a murderer and soon becoming his next victim? And who knew what had happened to the detective or my parents, for that matter.

I looked down at the orange linoleum and squeezed my eyes shut.

God. If You're there, please help me.

It was probably the shortest prayer ever prayed, but I didn't have a lot of time.

John X was looking at me again, head slightly tipped, eyes thoughtful. "So, Kate Carter, what should we do now?"

I shrugged. "You could let me go." It was worth a shot.

"Ah. See, I could. And I probably should. But you know I can't do that," he said, smoothly.

I nodded, my heart pounding. It had been five and a half minutes.

Where was the FBI?

DJ had stopped pounding on the door. He just stared at us through the window.

John X sighed. "Well, now, Kate Carter, I probably should do what I came here to do," he said.

Apparently, John X liked both my first and last name.

I looked at him and then back at the window. DJ was gone and I felt a mix of relief and panic. On the one hand, if he was working with John X, then I was glad he'd left.

On the other hand, now it was just the two of us.

And John X was pulling a small black gun from his pocket. He set it on the table between us and sighed again. "Such a waste of talent," he muttered. He looked over at me. "I hope you realize that I hate to do this."

I swallowed hard. I wasn't ready to die. I didn't know what came next. Heaven? A weird mix of memories? Eternal napping?

I heard tires crunch on the driveway right then. John X looked out the front window and frowned. "Hmm," he said.

I don't know what came over me. I grabbed the gun from the table and bolted for the front door. I had just gotten the top lock open when John X tackled me from behind. I fell forward, clutching the gun to my chest and hitting my head hard on the front door.

People were yelling outside, "FBI! FBI!"

My head was ringing. I'd fallen on my knees right in front of the door. I reached up to unlock the second lock.

I heard the snap almost before I felt it. John X had hit my left wrist so hard, he'd broken it. I started crying in pain.

The door in front of me blistered right as the windows shattered, but didn't break. They were bulletproof, after all. I screamed.

I scooted to the wall by the door, still holding the gun in an iron grip with my right hand. John X was kneeling right in front of me, pulling his fist back, shaking his head, aiming for my face.

"Stop right there."

John X froze.

My dad stood there behind him, 9mm trained directly on John X's head, his legs spread in a shooting stance. He didn't even look at me, he just kept both hands on the gun and both eyes on John X.

"Hands on your head. Now."

Slowly, ever so slowly, John X lifted both hands and put them on his head, falling cross-legged to the floor.

The front door busted open and suddenly the place was swarming with men with guns. Dad didn't move. John X didn't move.

And I sure didn't move because the two of them were trapping me against the wall.

One of the men pulled a set of handcuffs from his back pocket and wrapped them around John X's wrists, yanking him up and pushing him outside. "You know what?" he was saying as he escorted John X out. "I'm not even going to read you the Miranda warning. I'm going to let you tell it since you know it so well."

"Kate," Dad said, dropping to his knees in front of me. "Oh, Katie." He gripped me in a short hug and then stood. "I need a doctor!" he yelled, looking at my quickly swelling and bruising wrist.

I still had John X's gun in an iron grip against my chest. "DJ," I muttered, tears still streaming down my face.

Dad nodded. "They arrested him before they broke in," he said.

I blinked and looked up at him. "How did you — ?" As far as I knew, there was only one way into the house and one way out. And the front door was it.

Dad shrugged. "I shattered the back window when they were making all the commotion in here."

"It was bulletproof," I said.

"You can only make glass bulletproof to a certain extent, Kate." The engineer in my dad was taking over. "I shot three holes in it and then used the tire iron from Kent's car to break it the rest of the way. See, bulletproof glass works because it has several layers and the layers absorb the bullet so it doesn't pierce all the way through. But it does damage the rest of the glass, because — "

I shook my head and interrupted, because quite frankly, at that moment, I didn't care. "Mom? Detective Masterson?"

"Both fine. DJ knocked Kent out and locked him in the shed before he tried to come get you. I guess he was planning on taking you away from here to keep John X from finding you." Dad was shaking his head.

Mom ran into the house then, panicking. "Kate! Kate!" she screamed, dropping to the floor beside me. "Are you okay? You're alive! Where's the doctor? Where's an ambulance?" She grabbed my face in both hands. "Don't worry, Kate, we're getting you into intense psychotherapy when we leave here!"

I was worried about that. Actually, no I wasn't.

I just smiled at my parents and sniffled back the tears. "Let's go home."

Chapter Twenty

TWO WEEKS LATER

THE BELL WAS RINGING AND I LAID MY MATH HOMEWORK on my teacher's desk. "Don't forget about the pop quiz Monday!" he yelled over the bell as we left.

Yay.

It was the last class of the day and I was officially done with school for the week. In three weeks, I was going to be officially done with school for the entire summer. I stopped by my locker to grab my other books.

"Hey."

I looked over. Justin.

"Hey," I said, closing my locker and stuffing the extra books into my backpack.

"Are you coming to church on Sunday?" he asked.

I nodded. "Pretty sure." We'd been last Sunday. We again went to the late service and missed out on hearing the multicolored choir and the amen-ers, but I did meet a few more people from school, and now they waved and stopped to talk to me in between classes.

I had more friends than just Maddy. My mom was thrilled.

She hadn't made me go to psychotherapy, but she did ask me to let her know anytime I started thinking about what happened at the little house in the woods.

And she started reading through Luke with me.

So far, this guy named Jesus had made some pretty huge claims about himself. I was curious if they were going to hold true. I couldn't really understand why God had answered my prayer at the house, but he had and I was willing to learn more about him.

Justin nodded. "Want to come study with me?"

I shrugged on my ridiculously heavy backpack, sighing. "I can't. I've got work."

"Oh. Okay."

He actually looked kind of sad.

"I can come tomorrow though," I said.

He grinned at me. "Sounds good. See you tomorrow, Kate."

And then he winked at me before he left.

My stomach twisted slightly, and I cleared my throat. There was no time to think about Justin right now. I was already late.

I ran for my car and tossed my backpack into the passenger seat. We'd gotten a huge check as reward money for finding John X, and Dad had used it to upgrade my car. "I guess it's fine for you to drive something a little newer," he'd said grudgingly one day when I got home from school. A two-year-old Jeep Wrangler sat in the garage.

Now I couldn't help grinning as I drove to work. The sun was shining, the birds were singing. I had the windows down and the breeze was rifling through my hair.

I pulled into a parking place and walked inside, waving at the front-door secretary.

"They're waiting for you in the conference room," she said, smiling at me.

I opened the door and Detective Masterson and Deputy Slalom

were both sitting in the conference room. Detective Masterson stood and smiled shortly at me.

"Hi, Kate. How was school?"

"Fine. I actually —"

Deputy Slalom cut in then, stripping off his sports coat and rolling up his sleeves. "That's great, Kate, but we don't have time for pleasantries today. We've got a new witness for you, and this case is a doozy. Started in Arkansas and now this creep is moving north."

I sat down at the table, took a deep breath, smiled at Detective Masterson, and nodded at Deputy Slalom.

It was going to be a great summer.

Normal.

Acknowledgments

To my parents — Doug and Susan Mangum, thank you for loving me, raising me, and giving me the gift of a crazy imagination. I've always loved you, but I never appreciated you fully until we had Nathan! Thank you for everything you've done for me!

To my family — Bryant, Caleb, and Cayce Mangum; Greg, Connie, Allen, Vicky, Tommy, and Ashlee O'Brien: thank you for the laughs, the prayers, and for encouraging me. I am so blessed to have you as my family. I love you all!

To my friends — Clint and Leigh Ann Trebesh, Eitan and Kaitlin Bar, Mario and Elisa Martinez, Greg and Jen Fulkerson, Barb Walker, Shannon Kay, and my wonderful friends at Mars Hill ABQ — thank you for being such an incredible blessing in my life!

To the friends I've made at Zondervan, particularly Jacque Alberta — thank you! My agent, Steve Laube — thanks for helping me find a home for this novel.

Finally, to my Lord and Savior Jesus Christ — may everything I write be a way to draw closer and closer to You.

Discussion Questions for Sketchy Behavior

1. From the beginning, Maddy and Tyler have a dramatic relationship. And according to Kate, Tyler is a jerk. Why do you think Maddy and Tyler keep getting back together?
2. Kate's entry into forensic sketching is a little … sketchy. If you were Kate, how would you have reacted to the news that your art teacher had you draw a wanted criminal and the police knew about it? Do you think Miss Yeager and Detective Masterson's idea was worth the risk? Why?
3. Kate's brother, Mike, is never around. In fact, except for the time Kate's "big arrest" was on the radio, he never calls to find out how his sister is doing. How did this affect your opinion of Mike? Do you think he was aware of everything that was happening in South Woodhaven Falls?
4. Kate has a dating incident that will not be spoken about, ever. What do you think that event could be?
5. Even though she's in a lot of danger, Kate handles her sudden fame and her fear of John X with humor. If you were her, how would you have reacted? Do you think her humor in this situation is a coping mechanism, or is it just who she is? Why?
6. When Kate decides to grab her sunglasses during the parade, it ends up saving her life. Do you think that was more than a coincidence? What moments throughout the book seemed like coincidences at the time, but wound up becoming very important later?
7. Throughout the book DJ is a major person in Kate's life, living at her house as a bodyguard and interacting with her and her family in an almost brotherly way. Based on his characterization, did his past come as a shock to you? Why do you

think DJ was involved with the case and showed up at the FBI hideout? What do you think will happen to DJ?

8. Kate's mom decides that the family needs to attend church because "we need all the help we can get right now" (p. 60). What do you think of her mom's thought process? Do you know anyone who thinks the same way? What would you say to them?

9. In your opinion, why does Kate take the summer forensic sketching job after everything that happened with John X? Would you want Kate's job? Why or why not?

10. What do you think will happen between No-Longer-Silent Justin and Kate? What would you *like* to happen?

Check Out These Books
by Nancy Rue in the Real Life Series

Four girls are brought together through the power of a mysterious book that helps them sort through the issues of their very real lives.

Motorcycles, Sushi & One Strange Book

Boyfriends, Burritos & an Ocean of Trouble

Tournaments, Cocoa & One Wrong Move

Limos, Lattes & My Life on the Fringe

Also available in ebook and enhanced ebook versions.
Available in stores and online!

Talk It Up!

Want free books?
First looks at the best new fiction?
Awesome exclusive merchandise?

We want to hear from you!

Give us your opinions on titles, covers, and stories.
Join the Z Street Team.

Visit zstreetteam.zondervan.com/joinnow
to sign up today!

Also—Friend us on Facebook!

www.facebook.com/goodteenreads

- Video Trailers

- Connect with your favorite authors

- Sneak peeks at new releases

- Giveaways

- Fun discussions

- And much more!